I'VE HAD TROUBLE SLEEPING LATELY

& NINE OTHER
UPSETTING STORIES

PABLO ALFIERRI

For
Jack & Maxine

Two people who always believe in what I do.

When I was ten or eleven, I was at the beach, moseying around with a pink butterfly net I had received as a recent birthday gift. I'd spent some time trying to capture bugs to no avail; sand flies, beach moths *(are they a thing?)*, and at one point I even tried to capture a seagull. My endeavour to befriend a wild creature came up short, so I had decided to explore the rock pools instead, wondering perhaps whether I could catch a fish, or a crab, just something to take home with me to cuddle in bed later that evening.

Knee-deep, I waded through a particularly mossy, dark pool where I spotted a strange, soft mass hiding under a rock. I had no idea what it was, only that it was moving. A sort of mollusc, or sea slug. I watched it for a while, mesmerised by how it slithered along the shadow so seamlessly.

I wanted to see its underside, to figure out how it moved, maybe see if it had a face, maybe see if it would smile up at me. I took my small butterfly net and tried to flip it over, but I was too rough. I had dug the metal rim of the net into its flesh without understanding how fragile it was, cutting it clean in half. The rock pool immediately filled with blood. I had never seen such a thing. I had never felt more petrified. Initially, the fear was that stark visual: being a child, knee-deep in a pool of red. But that fear was quickly overshadowed by a much darker thing: guilt. The realisation that I had done that. I had killed a thing that bled.

For a long time, I thought that memory stuck with me because of the gore. But as I've struggled to finish this book over the last year, obsessing over every sentence, terrified of letting it go, I've realised it's about something else entirely. It's about the fear of ruining something fragile. The thing is, I have so many weird little ideas that I've kept hidden under a rock for years. I left them in the dark because I was scared. Scared that if I dragged them out, they would be judged. Scared that they weren't ready. Scared that by trying to capture them perfectly, I would just end up being that clumsy kid with the net again, destroying the very thing I wanted to share. These stories are the things I've been hiding. I am terrified to show them to you. But I'm handing you the net anyway. I truly hope you enjoy them, and please feel free to share your thoughts with me.

Thank you for reading,

Pablo

I

I'VE HAD TROUBLE SLEEPING LATELY

i've had trouble sleeping lately

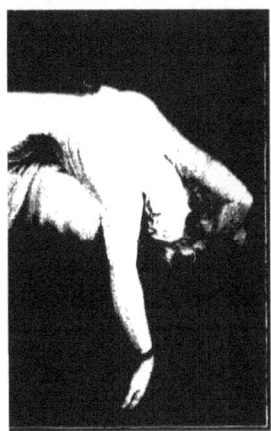

The Nightmare by Henry Fuseli (1781)

THE TILES PRESS HARD AGAINST HER BACK. That is what brings Asha back first. Back to her apartment, back to her body. The second is the trickle of water, lukewarm, trailing down her spine. She is cross-legged on the floor of the shower, eyes locked to the shadow of the drain as it swallows the remnants; it slurps, drinking it in, savouring the mix of water, soap, and blood. She has been here before, a long time ago, she remembers now. She does not want to remember, so she blinks, very hard. She focuses on the frosted window through the rise of weak steam. It's morning.

She struggles to pull herself up, knees wobbly as she twists the creaky tap shut. She steps out onto the bathmat and catches her reflection in the cabinet mirror. She is naked, wet, shivering, but not from feeling cold.

The water washed most of it away, while she was checked out, but she missed spots; there is a smear of dried blood on her chin, and a red line tucked under the curve of her left breast. She wipes them away with a damp thumb, then she pushes the window open, the glass shuddering in its old frame. A breeze drifts through. It catches the dampness on her cheeks. It feels good, but there's no relief. She looks at her reflection again. She does not remember coming here.

She remembers the bedroom.

She remembers the weight.

She remembers swinging her arm until it went numb.

She remembers the blood. So much blood. And then nothing. A gap.

Her phone is sitting on the edge of the sink. *Why?* She remembers the tap water rushing over the screen. She remembers the satisfaction of watching it fall silent. She stares at it now. It's utterly black, but soon flickers to life, as if cued by her gaze. Notifications fill the screen, one after another: MISSED CALL. MISSED CALL. MISSED CALL.

MUM. MUM. MUM. Seventeen calls. Asha watches, not reaching for it. She just watches.

***

Hours earlier, or longer, she can't be sure anymore, she had been in that same spot. Not bloodied, not yet, but not clean either. Far from it. She hadn't slept in so long, the edges of her days had started bleeding into each other. Her nights, pooling into one endless thing. Usually, the visits (that's what she called them), came only when she was really worn down. It waited for her sleep debt to rise, for her defences to weaken, and then they'd pass. A few bad nights, then weeks, sometimes even months, of nothing. She'd learned to live with it the way you learn to live with any chronic thing. It was there, and then it was gone, and the world kept turning. But this time was different. It kept coming. Every single *fucking* time she closed her eyes. First came the pressure on her chest. Then the figure in the frame. Watching her.

She had grown used to its presence, but more than that, and far more importantly, she had grown used to its stillness. As a child, Asha had convinced herself it was a statue, a sentinel guarding her as she slept. She used to whisper *goodnight* to the empty spot where it would manifest the moment she closed her eyes. As she got older, it would appear more frequently, particularly present during her teenage years, but always just standing there, just outside the door. Asha stopped saying *goodnight* to the thing after a while. Maybe that's why it changed recently. First, a head turn. Then, the twitch of its long, grey fingers. The shifting of weight from one foot to the other. It had never moved before. Maybe it was sick of the game, of standing just out of reach while she lay there frozen, screaming inside her skull. It had finally decided that watching wasn't enough anymore. It wanted in, and it was coming, and there was nothing she could do about it.

She tried to stay awake. When she returned home from work, exhausted from lack of sleep, she sat on the lounge with the television on. She watched a red-headed woman with a squeaky laugh demonstrate blenders. The volume was loud. Very loud. Loud enough so that the silence didn't have a chance to play tricks on her. A pedestal fan rattled by her feet, a damp cloth draped over the back of it. It hung there, now warm to the touch, the fan pushing the same hot air around the room in a useless, muggy loop. She watched television screen until her eyes begged for relief. There was nothing she wanted more than to close her eyes and finally rest. But the lounge room had too many shadows: the corners, the hallway, the darkness of the kitchen. It could be standing in any of them and she wouldn't even know.

"Well, of course it can!" the red-headed woman said enthusiastically, demonstrating how the blender could pulverise frozen coconut in mere seconds. In that moment, the cloth from the fan slipped loose, brushing across Asha's toes. She jerked her legs back, stomach dropping. *Just the cloth. Just the fan.* She pressed her hand against her chest, forcing her heart to slow. On the television, the red-headed woman was now drinking the coconut, in smoothie form, thick and white. Asha watched the woman's throat contract with each gulp. Then a big smile. Big and wide. Her teeth were far too perfect and white against the coconut milk on her upper lip. The living room suddenly felt open and exposed. She needed tighter walls, somewhere smaller.

The bedroom, she told herself. The bedroom would be safer. So she lay on top of the sheets, her sweaty back sticking to the fabric, staring at the ceiling fan going around and around and around and around and around and around and around and around. She tried to count the rotations. Tried to keep her mind on something other than the doorway. *Try distracting yourself before sleep*, Dr Greene had said. *Focus on something repetitive. Something calming. Try meditating.* Her eyes grew heavy. Although, the moment the room started to feel distant, the moment she felt herself slipping into unconsciousness, terror ripped through her. Her body jerked awake, pulse roaring through her ears, every muscle rigid. It was coming. If she slept, it would step inside. She couldn't stay there either. She went to the bathroom, because it was small and lockable. She sat, and she waited, and she fought sleep as hard as she could.

The hour had slipped past midnight and kept going, the world outside stopped moving and the silence felt like a held breath. Her body was screaming for relief: eyes burning, limbs heavy and strange, thoughts falling apart at the seams. She could sleep there, on the tiles. It felt cooler than the bedroom. She could close... her eyes... for just... a few minutes... and feel... some... relief. But the door was locked and it was coming and it would be locked inside with her. Her eyes jolted open again. She slapped herself, hard. Then she started to cry.

She just wanted to sleep. So desperately just wanted to *fucking* sleep. To lie down and let go and sink into nothingness. She would have traded anything for it. Her phone was in her hand now. She had been watching the screen, willing herself to make a decision. Even as she pressed the name, she knew it was a mistake.

Her mother, Catherine, would panic. It had been two years since she'd seen her. Asha knew she would get in the car and drive, and she would not stop until she was standing on Asha's doorstep. And she knew she wouldn't come alone. Asha's jaw tightened. She could see it so clearly. Her mother's old Holden pulling up outside her building, the passenger door opening, that tall figure standing. The grey hair with that soft voice, and those hands. She couldn't think about it. Not now. *TAP*. She'd done it. She'd actually done it. She had pressed the button and let the phone ring, *TRRLL ... TRRLL ...* and now her mother would know. After all this silence, all this distance. It was all completely erased, *TRRLL ... TRRLL ...* because she was tired, because she was scared, *TRRLL ... TRRLL ...* because she was so fucking weak. She had torn it all down with a single phone call. *Idiot.*

TRRLL ... TRRLL ...

The word rang through her: *Idiot. Idiot. IDIOT.*
TRRLL ... TRR—

Voicemail. Catherine's voice, cold and formal, asking the caller to leave a message. Asha hung up. What kind of message would she leave? *I think it wants in. Mum, it's coming for me. It moved, Mum. It moved. I think you might have been right all along and I can't bear it.* No. She couldn't give her that. Couldn't give her the satisfaction of being right, even if it meant sitting alone on the bathroom floor until she completely lost her mind. She scrolled to another name: Dr Greene. The number was still there from when the receptionist had made her save it. *In case you have questions. In case you need reassurance. Dr Greene wants you to know you can call any time. Any time.* Asha hovered over the name. She could call. She could hear the clinical voice explain it all again. The hallucinations. The brain just waking up before the body. She could let science wash over her like cool water.

I've had trouble sleeping lately. She had said that to Dr Greene. To so many faces. The words meant nothing anymore. There was the GP who scribbled a prescription before Asha had even finished talking. The psychiatrist who asked about her childhood, then handed her a referral to some specialist that cost more than two months rent. The sleep clinic technicians with their wires and electrodes and managed voices saying: *sleep, just sleep, sleep and relax and sleep and breathe.* And the medications. God, the medications. The cabinet above the sink was full of them. None of which could keep the shape out of her doorway. She had done the therapies, the meditations, the sleep hygiene cleanses. She had tried to imagine a safe place, to relax and breathe, while the thing stood watching from the door, waiting to get in. She tapped the screen. Dr Greene. It didn't even ring. Straight to voicemail. A recorded voice reciting office hours. *If this is a medical emergency, please hang up and dial 000.* Asha lowered the phone and stared at the black screen.

Somewhere outside, a motorbike tore down the street. The sound swelled and then faded. Then nothing again. The frustration was unbearable. A betrayal of her own body. Her own mind. But it… no. She couldn't allow herself to even think about it. But it could be. What if it was? A ghost? A monster? Was it even real? Was she even awake?

The phone started buzzing:

MUM. *BUZZ.* MUM. *BUZZ.* MUM. *BUZZ.*

She answered. She didn't even decide to; her thumb just moved, and then the phone was at her ear and her mother's voice was flooding in. "Asha? Asha, darl, is that you? Oh my goodness, are you there? Talk to me. Please, talk to me." Catherine's voice was cracking. She'd been crying, or was about to.

"I'm here," Asha barely whispered.

"Oh, thank God. Thank God. I saw the missed call and I just knew. I felt it in my heart. The Lord woke me and I just knew something was wrong. Are you alright? Where are you? Tell me where you are. I can't believe it's actually you."

Asha's legs pulled up towards her chest. She pressed her back harder against the tiles. She could tell her mother how scared she was. How she needed her. That she was prey, and it was coming.

"It's back. Mum, it's back and it... it moved. My sleep. I can't sleep. I can't..." She wiped the tears from her cheeks.

"Asha?"

"I'm fine. I shouldn't have called. It's late."

"Don't you…" Catherine's voice dropped, the tone she used when Asha challenged her, one of cold calculation. "Don't you dare dare do that. You call me after all this time and you expect me to just… what? Go back to sleep? Pretend you never called? You rang for a reason. So tell me where you are. Give me your address. I'll come to you." She paused. Thinking. Not for long. She made her decision. "Father George and I, we can help you. We can finally help you."

Heat flushed through Asha.

"I don't need help."

"You do. You know you do. You just won't admit it to yourself. For goodness sake, Asha, I want to help you. This *thing* that's happening. It's always been there. Since you were a baby, Asha. The way you used to scream in your cot. Do you remember? When you were five, the way you would point at the corner of your room and cry. You'd say 'Mummy! Look! Mummy! Who's that Mummy!' I knew then. We've always known."

"Mum, stop."

"It's a demon, Asha. It followed you there, to that city, wherever you are, because you ran from God and it knows. It knows you're unprotected. It knows you ran from me. Just tell us where you are."

Asha gripped the skin of her thigh. She could see it; the hands, the weight of them. She could smell it too; eucalyptus and licorice.

"I have to go."

"No. No, you listen to me. We're going to pray. Right now. Together."

"Mu— Catherine, please."

"Repeat after me. Heavenly Father, I come before you—"

Asha stood, her legs wobbled but held. Her mother's voice continued in that familiar cadence of prayer she'd endured ten thousand times. She twisted the tap on the sink, water rushing out. She placed the phone beneath it as Catherine's voice gurgled, then drowned to nothing. She watched the water run over the phone. How it flowed across the black glass in thin sheets, finding the edges, slipping into the seams. The screen flickered with a pale blue glow, then it went dark. It was so simple. A moment ago it had been so alive with her mother's voice, and now it was just a dead object, quiet. She could have stood there forever, letting the cold numb her fingers, staring into the void of that black peace. But instead, she fished the dead phone from the sink and set it on the edge of the basin.

She found herself in the kitchen. It wasn't as cool there, but it was just as dark. She fetched a glass and filled it with water, drinking it all in one long pull, feeling it trace a cool line down her throat. The relief lasted only seconds before the heat swelled in again. The apartment was stifling, the walls radiating the memory of the day's sun. She refilled the glass. Drank again. Stood there with her hip against the counter. Sleep felt like a foreign language, something intangible and utterly unimaginable. Her body was stuck between a state of adrenal-fuelled anger toward her mother's lack of understanding, and the all-encompassing fatigue of primal fear.

In the lounge room, the television droned on. That red-headed woman was still talking. It was getting louder. The words started blending together. The studio audience laughed. *When had there been an audience? Why was there an audience?* The sound swelled, pressing in on her, all around. L o u d e r: *WOW! IT'S SO SMOOTH! YUM!* L o u d e r: *HAHHAAAHHHAA!* Asha's hand trembled. The glass nearly slipped from her fingers. The noise was inside her head now, the woman's voice and the blender and the laughter all mixing into a single piercing frequency, until: *BZZT.* OFF. The silence crashed down with the piercing ring of white-noise. The apartment was completely still.

Then she felt it: a touch. On her knee. The pressure of fingers. The way it lingered, just a moment too long, so deliberately. The glass slipped from her hand. It shattered against the tiles, water splashing across her bare feet. She didn't move. She stood there, frozen, staring down at the scattered shards. She knelt down slowly, carefully picking up the pieces, the larger shards first. She placed them in her palm, one by one, feeling the edges press against her skin. She squeezed. She bled. She stopped. When she was done, she dropped them into the bin. Then she got a cloth and wiped up the water, pressing it into the cracks. As she wrapped the cloth around her hand, she knew. Even as she wrung the cloth out, she knew: the glass wasn't all gone. There were still pieces there, somewhere. Tiny fragments, invisible and hiding, waiting for a bare foot. And now they were probably inside her hand too, festering, clawing their way to the surface. Demanding to be remembered.

She went to the bedroom. She didn't want to, but the bathroom was ruined, tainted by her mother's voice, and the kitchen held the ghost of that touch inside tiny shards of glass. The room was even hotter than it had been earlier. She lay down on the bed. Again. The ceiling fan spun above her, again. But she didn't count this time. She thought: *Fuck it. Fuck it. Fuck all of it.* Her mother wanted her to pray? *Fine.* What else was there? The pills didn't work. The doctors didn't help. None of it had kept the thing from her doorway. Maybe Catherine was right. Maybe she had always been right. The words came slowly at first. She hadn't prayed since she was a teenager. Since the last time those hands had been laid on her and she'd been told she was cleansed.

Our Father, who art in heaven. Hallowed be thy name.

The syllables felt foreign.

Thy kingdom come. Thy will be done. On earth as it is in heaven.

She didn't believe it. She didn't believe any of it. But she was so tired.

Give us this day our daily bread. And forgive us our trespasses.

Let it come, she thought. Whatever it was. Let it come. She was too exhausted to fight anymore.

As we forgive those who trespass against us.

Her body was sinking. The mattress was swallowing her.

And lead us not into temptation. But deliver us from evil.

Her thoughts began to blur. The room felt distant and enormous.

For thine is the kingdom, the power, and the glory. For ever and...

She slept.

And instantly, she knew she had made a mistake.

She tried to move her hand and found it had fused to the mattress. Her legs were stone, her chest pinned beneath something immense and invisible. Her mind awake, her body dead asleep. *No. No, no, no.* Panic flooded her. She screamed but no sound came. Her jaw was welded shut. Her lungs could only draw the shallowest of breaths, tiny sips of air that weren't enough. A sound, low and wet. Something breathing through waterlogged lungs. It was coming from the doorway. Her eyes, the only part of her that obeyed, snapped open, straining to adjust in the dark. It was there. Standing just outside of the room, like it always was, taller than the frame. Thin, gaunt, and so pale. The skin was the colour of old putty, stretched crudely over slant bones.

It was naked. She could see its penis, small and shrivelled, hanging between its legs. The arms were too long by a good thirty centimetres, the shoulders too narrow for the width of the hips, the neck extending up and up. *Please. Please don't move. Don't move. Stay there. Let me sleep. Just watch me while I sleep, like you did when I was a little girl, remember? Please. Please. Please.*

It bent at the knees. Its long body folded downward, its head dipping beneath the frame, and Asha understood for the first time just how tall it truly was. Not just taller than the doorway, taller than anything that should exist. The movement was silent, its shoulders unfolding as it rose back to its full height inside the room. One foot, then the other. It was inside now. This was the closest it had ever come to her. She wanted to scream. She *was* screaming. She wanted to run.

She *was* thrashing. But her body was not hers. She could only watch as it moved. She couldn't even look away, her eyes now betraying her as much as her paralysed limbs. It stood there, scanning the space. First the bedside table. Then the wardrobe. Finally, it stopped. Its gaze fixed on the wooden crucifix hanging above her head. It had hung there since the day she moved in. She hadn't put it there for faith, she had put it there out of habit, and as it stared at the cross, something strange happened. Her terror began to fade. Her eyelids grew heavy. *No. Not now.* The creature was finally inside, and her mind was choosing this moment to betray her. She fought it. She strained against the weight pressing down on her. But the harder she struggled, the faster she sank into sleep. *No. Stay awake. It's coming. It's finally coming and you need to see, you need to be ready.*

But she couldn't. Her eyes closed.

The bedroom dissolved around her, and she was somewhere else. She was young, and she was sitting on the floor of the lounge room. The carpet was scratchy under her bare legs. The television was on. In the adjoining kitchen, she could hear her mother and her mother's friends, the clink of glasses and the shuffle of cards. The women laughed at something. Her mother's laugh was the loudest. Asha was supposed to be in bed, but she had come out for a glass of water, and she had lingered. She didn't want to go back to her room, she didn't want to be alone in the dark.

The smell of eucalyptus and liquorice. The click of a Fisherman's Friend lolly rattling against teeth. A hand on her knee. She kept her eyes on the television. *Good girl.* A cartoon.

A yellow and red bird flying through the sky. *Such a good girl, God loves you, good girl.* The weight of the hand, pressing on her leg, and then moving. Asha looked towards the kitchen. Her mother was standing in the doorway, a glass of wine in her hand. She was watching. *We will cleanse this, hm? We will cleanse it for you.* She was a shadow. She could see. She had to see. Catherine smiled. And then she turned and went back to her cards. *Good girl, no crying.*

The dream shifted. She was older, carrying a backpack down the hallway. It was late and very dark. The old carpet groaned beneath her feet as she crept. She winced with each sound, certain that the next step would be the one that woke her mother. But she kept moving. She had to keep moving. If she stopped, she would lose her nerve, and she would stay in that house forever. The front door was the hardest part. The lock was old and sticky. She held her breath as she gripped the metallic switch. *CLICK.* Nothing. No stir. No sound from her mother's room. She stepped outside. Her car was parked on the street, already loaded with her things. Everything she owned: a few boxes of clothes, books, movies, vinyls, and paintings she did when she was in high school. She was halfway down the front path when she heard it. *CLICK.* Asha turned. Her mother was standing at the door. The same shadow. Still as the moon. She wasn't calling out. She wasn't running to stop her daughter from leaving. She just stood there, watching. Asha waited for her to do something. To cry: *don't go.* To give her any reason to stay. Catherine didn't move. Not a single step. She turned her head slightly, shifted her weight, but she never left that doorway.

Asha got in the car, her hands shaking so violently she could barely fit the key in the ignition. The engine turned over, loud in the quiet street, and she pulled away from the kerb without looking back. She drove until the house was gone, until the whole town was just a smear of distant lights in the rearview mirror. She didn't cry. She thought she would, but she didn't. She just drove, hands stuck to the wheel, eyes fixed on the dark stretch of road ahead. She never went back. She never called. She deleted the voicemails without listening. She built a life out of silence and distance, and she told herself it was better this way. And for a while, she almost believed it was.

Asha's eyes snapped open. The bedroom. The heat. The smell of her own sweat. She was back. But the doorway was empty, and she was still trapped inside her own body. For one desperate second, she thought it was over. Maybe the prayer had worked. Maybe it had banished the thing back to wherever it crawled out from. That was until she looked at the foot of the bed. It was there. Perched. Its limbs folded in like a cat. Its knees jutted upward, rising high past its shoulders. Its fingers, impossibly long, were hooked into the flesh of its brow, prying its own eyelids wide open to reveal small, glistening black beads.

In the doorway, it had always been half-swallowed by shadow. But now it was here, and she could see everything. The eyes did not blink. They *could* not blink. It was a taunt. A cruel pantomime of what she had tried to do. *You wanted to stay awake?* it seemed to say. *This is how you stay awake, little girl.* Asha's desperate mind scrambled for the prayers, but nothing came. The words disintegrated before they could form. Then it moved, unfolding itself from its crouch. It placed one long-fingered hand onto the mattress, then the other. Asha felt the dip, the sag of the springs under a weight far heavier than that frame should allow. It began to crawl up the bed towards her, its torso settling over her stomach, driving the last of the air from her lungs. Its bony thighs pinned her own. The creature lowered its head, its face hovering just above hers. Its dark mouth opened, revealing brown teeth, the size of Tic Tacs, gapped between bloodied, rotted gums. Its tongue emerged, thick, leathery, hanging in the air before her. Asha squeezed her eyes shut. *Please, stop. Good girl.* Rough, yet slick, it moved across her lips, forcing them apart.

She tasted something she couldn't name at first. Old, earthy, like flowers left too long. But then: liquorice, eucalyptus. Its tongue was a heavy, rotting weight. It thrashed against the back of her teeth and slicked across the roof of her mouth, hunting for her own tongue as it unconsciously curled back in a desperate, gagging retreat. It was in that moment that something inside Asha broke open. The terror was still there, but there was now a rage, a fire, using the fear as its fuel. The muscles in her arm began to knot and tear with immense heat. A tremor started in her hand, her fingers gripped, her toes curled, and with a roar torn from her chest, Asha wrenched herself free. The paralysis shattered instantly. In one swift motion, she lunged upward, her hand shooting toward the wall above the headboard, fingers closing around the wooden crucifix. Her fingers wrapped around it like it was the only solid thing left in the world. She tore it from its hook, plaster dust showering down.

One moment she was pinned beneath the creature, the next, the world had inverted. She straddled its waist, her thighs clamping down on those sharp hips, and she raised her right hand high above her head. The crucifix was a perfect fit for her fist. She brought it down. The first blow caught the creature across the face, the sound a deep, wet thud. A cool mist sprayed her cheek. The creature didn't cry out. It absorbed the blow. She struck again, at the hollow of its throat. Her shoulder screamed. She ignored it. Again, at its chest. Something cracked under the impact. Maybe wood, maybe bone.

Again. She was sobbing now, gasping for air between each swing.

Again. Her arm was burning. The crucifix was slick in her grip.

Again. She couldn't stop. She didn't want to stop. The creature's limbs moved, but not to attack. Its long grey fingers reached upward, and she flinched, expecting claws. But the hand didn't strike. It rose, trembling, and hovered in the air between them. It was shielding its face.

Asha hesitated. For one fraction of a second. But she saw the gesture for what it was. *A trick. A final deception.* The same venom her mother had told. *We only want to help you. We only want what's best.* She brought the crucifix down harder. The creature's face was a ruin now.

Its mouth was split down to the chin, flesh hanging. One of its eyes had been reduced to a pulpy mass, leaking a dark liquid down the side of its skull. Small teeth lay scattered on the pillow. She could see bone beneath the mess of its chin, where the skin had peeled. And still it didn't fight. Still it lay beneath her, absorbing each blow. Again and again and again, harder and again, harder, again, again, again, again. She saw the mouth open, the jaw hanging wrong, dislocated, but trying to move. Not to scream, but as if to speak. A bubble of black swelled between what was left of its lips. And with a final cry, she drove the bottom edge of the splintering crucifix directly into that open mouth, felt it scrape against the teeth that remained, felt the soft resistance of the tongue, and then the harder stop of the back of the throat. She leaned her full weight onto it, driving it deeper, feeling the cartilage give way, hearing the wet pop as the wood pushed through. She plunged the cross with what little adrenaline she had left, until the body stopped twitching, until the only movement was the spread of darkness pooling beneath its head.

A final tremor ran through its body, a spasm that lifted them both from the mattress for a single moment, then it collapsed.

Asha remained poised above it, her thighs loosening their grip, her chest heaving with sobbing gasps. Sweat and tears mingled down her cheeks as she attempted to slow her breath. The crucifix was still buried in the thing's mouth, her fingers locked around it so tightly she couldn't feel them anymore.

It was over. She had done it. She had fought the monster in the dark and she had won. God had answered her prayer. In that triumph, she almost wanted to laugh. She could feel it building inside, a bellow clawing its way up from her stomach. She wanted to call her mother and say *it was a demon and I killed it with my own hands. It's done. I won.* And she wanted to laugh with her mother, laugh until they both went numb and tears streamed and they would hug and cry and say how much they miss each other and how Catherine was right, but also wrong, and that yes, she should have stopped her from driving away, running away, all those years ago, but no, she didn't, and yes, she was so sorry and they would both meet for coffee and Asha would tell her how, yes, she was molested, no, she was raped, by the priest, their priest, and she would forgive Catherine, her mother, for allowing it to happen, for *wanting* it to happen, and they would then order fresh pastries and catch up on good old times as if time had not ticked at all, as if Asha had been sleeping fine this whole time, *i've been sleeping great lately*, she would say, and it would be as if Asha did not miss her mother at all, they would not talk about how Asha tried to kill herself last year, but got too scared because she was scared of going to hell, and it was okay now because it was in the past and the vanilla slice tastes so fresh and creamy, they would not talk about all of the bad things because she would laugh, she would laugh with her mother and everything was going to be fine.

Magpies. Carolling outside, in the big tree through the window. Signalling dawn approaching. She loved, loves, the sound of magpies.

Slowly, shakily, she pushed herself off the thing. Then off the bed entirely. She never took her eyes off it. It lay twisted and broken, half on the bed and half on the floor. She sat there for a long time, in the corner of her room, her back against the wall, just breathing. The light of morning crept in, pushing back the shadows. It touched the wardrobe by the bathroom door, then the leg of the bed, then the body.

She took a deep, rattling breath. She needed to see. She needed to look upon the face of the defeated demon in the clear light of day. Wiping the tears and blood and sweat from her eyes, she stood. And she looked. And as she looked, the magpies fell silent.

The skin was the first thing to change. What she had seen as grey and desiccated was now, in the new light, the flushed pink of living skin. Pale, yes, but not the pallor of a corpse. The pallor of something that had never needed the sun. What she had seen as an emaciated, ashen, skeletal frame, was now lean and graceful. The angles she had read as predatory were, in the growing dawn, something else entirely. It was the body of a young man, serene even in the violence she had forced upon him. Around the pulverised mess of his face, soft, golden curls framed what was left.

A trick. Her mind screamed. *A final deception.* It had to be. But the light kept coming. And the truth kept changing. She laid a trembling palm on its shoulder. The frame was unnaturally light. When she pushed, it rolled easily. She saw what had been hidden beneath, crushed against the floor: a wing. A mass of white feathers, layered with divine geometry. Or it had been, now it was ruined. The bone keeping it all together was snapped. The white plumage was matted with gore. She did not need to see the other one to know what she had done. Asha stared into the carnage, at the thing of impossible beauty she had destroyed, and as she did, a single feather shaken loose by the ceiling fan detached itself. It hung in the air for a moment, a white fleck in the light, before beginning its descent.

And there, in the place where God used to be, where God never was, perhaps even where God should have been, the only sound left was the soft whisper of that single feather landing on the floor, and the magpies outside, continuing their carols.

II

GORGEOUS

gorgeous

Narcissus by Caravaggio (c. 1597–1599)

PAIGE, THE RECEPTIONIST, was a twenty-something with raspberry red hair whose name tag barely clung to her polo. She didn't look up when I approached the counter. Her long, acrylic claws, each a different scream of pastel, clacked against her phone screen as she tapped away. She finally realised I was standing in front of her, setting the phone down with a sigh. Like, a proper sigh.

"Name?" she clipped. I wondered if she was the one who'd called this morning, delivering the news about my chlamydia with too much enthusiasm. Judging by Paige's general air though, it seemed doubtful.

"Kieran," I said. "Jankovski."

Her fingers danced across the keyboard.

"Medicare card."

"Wanna buy me dinner first?" I mumbled in a funny American accent. She didn't so much as blink. My faux smile quickly faded, as I slid the card across the counter under the clear plastic shield. She snatched it, tapped a few more keys, then slid it back.

"Take a seat. The doctor will call you out."

"Thanks." I said.

This Paige girl was a Scent. I usually liked those Types. They always had an 'over it' sort of attitude. Could you imagine it? Having an insanely well-attuned sense of smell? It would be exhausting; it's a Type I didn't envy. I was just grateful I'd showered and remembered deodorant. Though, I wondered if the deodorant was a bit much. It was a new brand I hadn't bought before: HYPER-MAX ULTRA DEODORANT

24-HOUR PROTECTION ULTIMATE DELUXE, or something. Maybe that was why she seemed so offended by my presence.

"Is it my deodorant?" I asked, half stepping into the waiting room. She was already back on her phone, swiping away. I pressed on: "It's a new one. Never used it, sorry. Does it stink?"

"Sorry?" She looked up. "What?"

"My smell. Is it too strong?"

"You're a Reader?"

I was offended by the question. It was rare, and kinda rude, for people to ask your Type straight-up like that.

"Yeah."

"Cool," she offered. She gave me what I could only assume was an incredibly rare smile. "No, you're fine." And she was back to her phone.

The waiting room was grim as all fuck, it had not been touched since the early 70s. Just a handful of red and green plastic chairs bolted to the floor, cracked and peeled at the edges. And the carpet, a faded abstract monstrosity on its last legs, was deeply stained and frayed in every corner. There were a few artificial monsteras scattered around too, caked in dust. Two older men sat at the far end of the chairs near the entrance. They were both hunched over, staring down at their phones. One was an Echo, the other, an Anchor. The Echo, maybe mid-fifties and a bit fat, gave me a soft smile as I passed to sit down. Echoes always knew when you needed a smile, but I wasn't really in the mood for one so I didn't give him one back. Plus, this was a clinic for gay people. If I were to return the smile, even out of politeness, he might think I was sexually interested in him, and by the heavens, I was far from it.

Across from me, another guy, roughly my age, sat engrossed in his phone too. His jaw was defined, his face clear and smooth beneath a spiralling mass of dark hair. He looked like Jacob, you know, the wolf guy from Twilight. But with curlier hair. His faded shirt, a vintage design of some national park somewhere, clung to a body of what looked like muscle and that frustratingly naturally-toned look. I noticed a bulge of veins along his bronzed forearms and hands, popping out while he tapped, a detail I always found particularly hot. He was the kind of effortlessly handsome that always seemed unfair. It pissed me off.

He glanced up. His impossibly black eyes met mine for a fraction of a second before I shot my head down, looking at nothing in particular. *Embarrassing. You're so embarrassing, Kieran. You were staring at him and he caught you.* I had just tried to read his Type, that was the only reason I was looking at him, I promise. But nothing came. I drew a complete blank. That rarely ever happened, not unless I was a few too many ciders deep, or really high, or really stressed out.

I like my Type, but being a Reader is a strange experience. It was an ability people wanted in theory, but not one that was truly desired. It was useful for service roles and therapy, and things like that. Jobs where you need to know how people are going to act, and more importantly, how they are going to *re*-act. That's why I'm so good at my job, customer service. If I read someone's Type, let's say for example they're an Adrenal, you have about ten minutes to fix their issue before they get overstimulated and need to go for a jog then punch something. Shit thing is though, Readers' abilities only manifest after puberty. Most Types develop at birth and attune, sharpening with age. Readers take a while to warm up. We were often mistaken for Typicals, which are those born without any Type, poor things. It meant a whole chunk of our formative years were spent feeling a bit... I dunno, lost? Different? It was like you'd missed the memo on something. There was a weird homesick feeling. Then when it finally decided to show up, there was a sense of loss for all those years spent feeling like everyone was growing pubes except for you. Could call it trauma, I guess, if you were feeling dramatic.

So I wondered if he was a Reader too, the hot guy across from me, and he'd caught me trying to decipher his Type. I found myself tapping on the yellow and black icon. Grindr. Maybe I could see if he was on there, figure out his Type listed on his profile. But before I could check, a fresh message was waiting for me. It was a headless torso with perfectly sculpted abs and huge, pinkish/grey nipples:

ANONYMOUS: *Hey. Got any more pics?*

He'd seen my profile picture. It was the one from the shoulders up, the one I took a few days ago because I'd lost more weight. My jawline was finally starting to appear, and my cheeks were less full. But this was always the next step, the demand for verification. The proof that my body was as desirable as the carefully curated face picture. I scrolled through my camera roll, entering the album where I stored my nudes and selected one. It was a bathroom mirror selfie. The light was as forgiving as possible, and my stomach was sucked in just enough to hide the worst of it. The stretch marks, pale and silvery on my hips, were still visible though. I didn't want to pretend like they didn't exist. But, god, my stomach looked like a deflated balloon, wrinkled and shrunken from where I'd lost the weight. I wondered if he'd notice straight away. I wondered if everyone in this clinic noticed. Yeah, whatever, let's send it. I hit the button. The small tick beneath the photo marked it as delivered. I watched and I waited.

One second.

Two.

Under his Type section it read ADRENAL.

My thumb moved.

Swift and economical.

Tap profile.

Scroll.

Block.

I had to beat him to the punch.

What was I going to do with an Adrenal anyway? They already get enough attention. *You deserve better. You'll find someone one day, I promise. You're disgusting. I fucking hate you. You're not eating today. Don't you dare fucking eat today.* I locked my phone. The screen went black and reflected a greasy, distorted image of my face back at me. At that exact moment, the handsome guy across from me looked up again. His eyes caught mine. This was a real look, not just a fleeting glance.

I knew he saw it all. He saw the ugliness I felt radiating off me like heat. I fought the urge to pull up my shirt and expose my soft stomach to him, to the rest of the world. I wanted to scream: *Yes. Here it is. Look at my disgusting stomach. Look at this skin. Look how it stretches! Woo!*

"Kieran Jankovski?"

A woman with dark, shiny hair appeared in the open doorway. She had a kind smile with beautiful teeth, introducing herself as Priya. She led me into a small treatment room dominated by an examination bed covered in crinkly blue paper. I sat on it as we entered. The paper crumpled under my weight. I perched there somewhat primly, like a woman waiting to be painted. I hadn't done this before.

"Oh, you can sit here," Priya said with a slight giggle. She gestured to a chair beside her desk. I felt a flush creep up my neck.

A silver wedding band was nestled on her left ring finger. I noticed it immediately. She was an Anchor. They always had their shit together. My last, and only boyfriend, was an Anchor, which meant he always had to be right. Always telling me how to spell things properly and how many meals to eat in a day. We lasted less than a year. His name was Brian, which didn't help.

"Alright, Kieran," she said, her tone similar to that of a yoga instructor. "Just the usual questions before we get to the treatment. Is that okay honey?"

I nodded. I loved people who used pet names like that. Honey, sweetie, darling, baby.

"Under the Type Disclosure Act of 2028," Priya began, "we're required to ask for your Type before we can offer any treatment. I understand it's a bit of a taboo subject, but if you're able to—"

"Reader," I said, getting it out of the way.

"Thank you." She typed a few notes, "and in the last three months, how many sexual partners have you had?"

The question landed with its usual dread. This wasn't because I felt shame for being gay, or for having sex, I'm no saint. It was the disbelief I had always braced for. The quiet judgment I saw flicker in their eyes. I imagined the gears turning in her head as she looked at me. She looked at this soft, unremarkable body, trying to reconcile it with the number.

"Five," I said.

I know, you don't believe me, trust me, I wouldn't either.

Her fingers danced across the keyboard. "All casual partners?"

"Yeah."

"And for those encounters, was a condom used every time?"

I pretended to think about it. I threw around a hum while my eyes drifted to a rainbow flag poster taped above the door. It said *WASH YOUR HANDS, KEEP OUR COMMUNITY SAFE!*

"Uh, I think so, yeah," I said. The lie rolled off my tongue easily. It was always no. The encounters were always brief and furtive. Dark rooms, saunas, even a park at night one time. Places where the shadows were kind and I could take what I could get. I thought about the guy from a few nights ago, the one who messaged me at two in the morning, the one who said *fuck you're hot, wanna meet me in the park, by the toilets?* Afterward, walking home, I got another few messages from him. *Sorry.* He'd said. *I thought you were fitter, sorry. My bad. Have a good night,* he'd said.

Priya just nodded. "Okay. Thanks." She turned from the screen. "So, for the chlamydia treatment, I'll give you an injection in your bum now, and then you'll—"

"Yeah all good," I blurted, cutting her off. She seemed taken aback.

"Sorry," I mumbled. I didn't want to hear about how to fix this stupid thing. I didn't care. I don't care. They were moments that meant nothing anyway.

"You will need to inform any partners from the last three months so they can get tested as well."

"No worries."

Later, after she'd placed a small cotton ball on the puncture in my buttock, Priya offered another kind smile. "It's important you don't have any sexual contact for the next seven days."

Her words drifted around me, distant, as if I were underwater. All I could think about was the drug coursing through my blood, fighting the bacteria like a war happening inside of me already. It all felt so foreign and foul. I deserved it.

"Thanks," I said. I pulled up my pants and did up my belt. The injection in my butt still felt a little tender. "That wasn't too bad."

Priya held out a small, clear bowl filled with colourful wrappers. "Do you want some condoms?"

I hesitated. "Bit late now? Huh?" I laughed. "No, I'm all set, I think. Thank you."

She nodded, smiled, and held the door open for me.

My heart was already quickening. I hoped he was still out there, Jacob, from the waiting room. Maybe he'd look up just as I emerged. Our eyes would meet properly this time, I'd offer a smile. A real one. I made my way toward the entrance, past the waiting area. My eyes swept immediately to where he'd been sitting. But the chair was empty. Only the two older men remained, hunched over in their seats. The Echo man looked up as I passed. He offered that smile again. *Creep.*

***

The following days blurred into a grey void of waiting. Waiting for the antibiotics to work. Waiting for the all-clear. Waiting for anything but the quiet of my apartment. I worked from home, so the boundaries between my living and working spaces had dissolved into a single monotone lately. I left the apartment only to force myself into the indifferent fresh Melbourne air.

The spare time I did have was spent on the lounge. The television was a meaningless buzz of The Real Housewives while I fell into the glowing void of my phone. Grindr was a wound I couldn't stop picking at. The brief thrill of a new message and the jolt of hope. Then the inevitable request for more photos, the silent gamble of sending them, the agonising wait, and then the crushing silence.

I'd often get out of bed most mornings and place my laptop precariously on my lounge. I'd open Fitness With Gal's YouTube channel and press play on whatever latest workout she was spruiking. This morning was 'lower-body sweat-a-thon'. I did the movements. I felt the loose parts of my body flip and flop when I moved along with her.

"Say it with me! More!" she'd scream.

"More!" I'd say back in a breathless whisper.

"Again! With me! More!"

"More!"

She was a Morph, although she marketed herself as an Echo. Her body was Adonis-like. Structured in a way that felt inhumane. People were catching onto these fitness influencers lately, especially the Morphs. They were often called out in the comments by Readers like myself.

After my workout, I'd often watch Gal's vlogs too, while preparing breakfast. By breakfast, I meant my antidepressant, my oral antibiotic, and a muesli bar. Some mornings, that was all I could keep down. In today's vlog, she was getting a morning coffee with Frank, her Grower boyfriend. Growers were at the top of the food chain, especially in the gay world, for self-explanatory reasons.

It seemed to be getting closer. I could feel it. Every workout, every video, every study of how their relationship worked. I'd eventually have what she has. *I will. I deserve it. Just eat less, work harder.*

My phone buzzed.

ANONYMOUS: *Hey handsome.*

I rarely replied to anonymous profiles. It was a risky mixed bag. Sometimes they'd be a secret hottie who was discreet for their own reasons. They might be looking for a taboo Type, they might be in a relationship, or perhaps they were looking for a discreet one-off encounter. I shouldn't reply, I deserve full transparency.

ME: *Hey :]*

ANONYMOUS: *I hope you're feeling good today. You deserve to feel good today.*

Weird, although the break in script was refreshing. My curiosity was piqued. It was rare to receive a message, without having initiated the conversation first.

ME: *Aw. That's really nice of you. You too. Do you have any pics?*

There was a pause. Enough time for me to head to the bathroom.

Afterwards, I looked at myself in the mirror. I realised I'd thrown up the antibiotic too. I took another one before he replied again.

ANONYMOUS: *[sent a picture]*

It was the fat guy, the Echo from the clinic. I blocked him immediately.

Later that afternoon, I was knee-deep in customer-care calls. The drone of complaints was a familiar soundtrack to my work day. My eyes, however, were drawn to a notification. A new message had popped up on Grindr. The profile picture wasn't a headless six-pack, which was a common sight. This was a face. A very handsome face. The profile name was Jack. Not Jacob. Jack. The guy from the clinic. *Holy shit.* My heart was doing backflips.

JACK: *Hey.*

"Excuse me? Are you even listening?" A shrill voice crackled in my headset. It was a woman named Briette, whose internet had been cutting out for the past two days.

"Sorry," I mumbled, already typing. "Just technical difficulties on my end. Yes, I'm still here."

ME: *Hey, how are you?*

"Well, you clearly aren't, because if you were, you'd know I've been explaining this for the fifth fucking time!" Briette huffed. "My modem lights are blinking red and then orange and then red again and then orange one more time!"

A moment later, Jack's response came through.

JACK: *Good, you?*

"Red, then orange, then red again," I muttered. My fingers were flying.

ME: *Good.*

I hit send.

"NO! Orange! Orange!" Briette roared.

"Oh, my mistake. Orange," I responded calmly. Even over the phone, I could read her Type. That was how attuned my skill had become over the years. She was a Blast. I loved them at parties for the sheer drama they brought. But when dealing with a Blast in a customer service role, you were guaranteed to hear at least a 'cunt' or a 'fuck' here and there.

As Briette continued her tirade, my focus drifted back to Jack's profile. It was pretty bare. Just a few blurry photos, but under the Type section, it read: GRIP.

A lie. I'd tried to read him back at the clinic and drawn a blank, which was almost unheard of for me. Grips were usually so easy to decipher. I'd never had a problem in the past. Not only were they easy to read through my own ability, but physically it was obvious too. It was in the constant use of gloves, or the subtle ways they held things. They did anything to stop their skin from adhering to surfaces. He wasn't wearing gloves.

Why would he bother lying about something so mundane? Grips weren't exactly sought after on the apps. Sure, they might be handy if you needed to scale a building, but for a hook-up?

"Alright, I've just initiated a remote reset on your modem," I said, cutting off Briette's latest complaint." It should be back online within five minutes. If not, please call us back and we can escalate the issue."

I clicked the call dead and pulled off my headset. My attention was entirely on Jack's profile now.

He continued initiating conversation, which I was not at all used to. It was usually me who pursued, me who complimented strangers with half their face covered in their profile photo, me who blamed myself when I didn't receive a response.

JACK: *I was going to ask for your number at the clinic, is that lame?*

ME: *Bullshit. You're a fucking liar, and I do not trust you.*

Delete.

ME: *Bullshit. You're fucking with me. Right?*

Delete.

ME: *Really?*

JACK: *Yes, really.*

ME: *Why?*

Delete.

ME: *That's sweet.*

Delete.

ME: *What are you up to?*

We talked for an hour. He told me what he did for work, a fully-fledged artist who got paid full-time to make art, full-time. It was hard to believe, but after tracking down his social media profiles, it was true. He didn't post any photos of himself, at all, only his artwork. He probably had a private account where he was followed by a tonne of hot boys, but whatever.

His artwork, if you'd even call it that, was scary. Really freaky statues and sculptures that looked like they were moulded out of actual flesh. I hate scary stuff. He posted a lot of poems and quotes and photography too, it all went over my head. Then, without skipping a beat, he steered the conversation to my Type.

JACK: *So, being a Reader. Is it tiring? Like, do you always have to be 'on'?*

I paused. Surprised by his curiosity. Most people just asked *what* my Type was.

ME: *It's not so much 'on' as it is background noise at this point. Like you know how a Scent can't just turn off their nose? It's always there. Most of the time I can tune it out, but some types just vibrate heaps loud. I dunno how to explain it, but I tune in, then out, if I want to.*

A beat passed before his reply came through.

JACK: *Haha, yeah. I had a Reader friend a few years ago. She said she always had trouble reading my type. Funny.*

Still lying. A Grip's energy was so easy to read. The mystery of him only deepened.

There was a lull in conversation. He stopped initiating. I tried to distract myself by playing Pinball Paradise on my computer, but it didn't work, my eyes kept straying back to my phone's lockscreen, notification-less.

After about twenty minutes, I said "Fuck it," and snatched the phone. I swiped it, opened our chat, and sent the pictures. The really bad ones too. The ones of my soft belly and my scarred hips. He was being so nice, and I had no idea how to respond, so it was easier to just get it out of the way now. He needed to see the truth. He wouldn't show me his, so I'd show him mine first.

The three dots appeared instantly. He was typing. This was it. I braced for the polite exit.

I walked to the bathroom. I knelt against the toilet, knees pressed into the tiles. I stared into the water. The phone sat on the floor beside me.

It buzzed.

I didn't look. I couldn't look. Another buzz. I counted to ten. Then twenty. Then I picked it up.

JACK: *Woah.*

I held my breath. I felt sick.

JACK: *You're gorgeous.*

I read the words again. Then again. *GORGEOUS.* I stood, still staring at the screen.

JACK: *Thank you for sharing. Are you free later tonight?*

My fingers flew across the screen before I could stop them.

ME: *Yes.*

JACK: *My address is [address]. Come over at like, eight?*

I stared at the message. *Wait.* Wait a minute. He saw it all. The really bad ones. The soft belly, the scarred hips, everything. And he still wanted to see me?

It didn't make sense. Every time I sent those photos, every single time, I'd be ignored. Or blocked. Or they'd send back something cruel, proving they'd only been polite because they hadn't seen the truth yet. This had to be a joke. Some kind of setup. Maybe he was laughing with his mates right now, screenshots already shared. Maybe the address was fake. Or worse, maybe it was real, and I'd show up to find a group of them waiting, phones out, ready to film the fat faggot who actually thought someone wanted him.

I should block him. Delete the app. Forget this ever happened.

But I didn't. I opened Google Maps and checked the address. Real. A suburb I knew. Not too far. My hands were shaking as I typed back.

ME: *See you at eight :)*

Delete.

ME: *See you later!*

Delete.

ME: *Sounds good, see you tonight.*

***

The Uber pulled up just before eight. The driver was older. When I got in, he turned around. "Kieran?"

You're fucking kidding me. The older guy. The Echo from the clinic.

"Yeah."

He turned back, hands on the wheel, and started driving. I'd forgotten my headphones like an idiot, like I'd never taken public transport in my entire life.

Please don't talk. Don't talk. Please.

"Lovely evening for it," he said as we stopped at a red light.

I gave a little "Mmm," my eyes fixed on some people sitting outside a bar laughing.

My phone was in my hand. I could unblock him, maybe he didn't notice. I wondered if he knew. If Echos could just... sense that sort of thing.

We drove in silence for a bit. Then:

"First date?"

My stomach dropped.

"Can be a bit nerve-wracking, but nothing to worry about." He said.

I stared out the window. He didn't sound angry. He didn't sound like anything.

"Yeah," I muttered.

"That's nice." He indicated left. "Hope it goes well."

I waited for him to say something. To call me out. To make some comment about the clinic, about seeing me there, about blocking him, about anything. But he just drove, humming quietly to a song on the radio I didn't know. It was a nice song.

"You look lovely, by the way," he said as we pulled into Jack's street. "Very put together. You'll be fine."

My throat tightened. *Is he actually still trying? Shut the fuck up.*

"Thanks," I said.

He pulled up to the address. I reached for the door handle.

"Kieran?" he said.

I froze.

"I–uh. I don't want to sound out of line, and I hope it's okay that I say this."

"I'm not into you man." I snapped.

He laughed. Not in a way of diffusion, or embarrassment, but a genuine laugh. "I'm not trying to… It's all good. I just. I felt you, at the clinic. It's all good. You have fun tonight, and stay safe. You'll be fine." He turned, his calm eyes locking with my frantic ones. He smiled.

I got out without looking back. The car idled for a moment before pulling away, and I stood there on the footpath.

I checked the address on my phone again, it was definitely the right place. Damn, artists must get paid well. I peered up at the old brick warehouse converted into apartments. Real hipster-type shit.

The lock sang a little harmony when I buzzed his apartment. "Come on up!" Jack's voice crackled from the intercom. I pushed open a large set of heavy glass doors, stepping into a concrete stairwell that smelled of cold metal and weed. The door at the top was ajar, spilling a yellowy-orange light onto the landing.

He was leaning against the doorframe like a Greek god welcoming a weary pilgrim. Barefoot, wearing a simple grey t-shirt and loose jeans. Fuck he was hot. Even better looking than I remembered.

"Hey," he said, voice echoing down toward me. "You made it."

"Yeah," I managed. Feeling suddenly shy.

He stepped back as I entered, pretending I wasn't utterly out of breath. I walked into a cavernous, intimately lit studio apartment. The ceiling was stupidly high, criss-crossed with old steel beams that were rusted in a way that looked intentional. A massive arched window with brass detailing looked out over the quiet inner-north neighbourhood. The place was a beautiful yet organised Pinterest-worthy mess of plants, art, books, and vintage furniture.

"Damn this is nice," I said. I spun around in a slow circle. And as my eyes scanned the room, I almost jumped out of my skin.

In the centre of the lounge area, on a low pedestal, sat a sculpture. One of his artworks. It was about the size of a person. A mass of twisting, writhing forms that hinted at limbs and a torso, but they stretched and contorted into an unnatural mass of flesh.

The surface of the statue was a swirl of pinks and deep reds. It glistened under the lighting, wet, like exposed flesh. I couldn't look away.

Ew.

My gaze snagged on a particularly gnarled leg, contorted as if in agony, its bones and skin flayed open like a strange flower.

"God," I breathed. Barely a whisper. "What *is* that?"

Jack's eyes followed mine. A low laugh rumbled in his chest. "Honestly, I forget that's even there sometimes, isn't that funny? "It's a bit intense, I know. But I love it."

I drew closer and circled the unsettling thing, taking in every disturbing detail.

He stepped a little closer to me. His presence was warm on my back. "It's just been here for so long now. It was one of the first ones I did. So it's like, just a piece of the place now." He gestured vaguely around the apartment. "The whole space sort of grew around it."

I turned to face him. He was closer than I'd realised. Smiling, a relaxed and easy smile. *Kiss me, please.*

"Drink?" he asked.

"Yeah. Thanks."

I watched him circle a large, wooden bench island in the kitchen area. A deep stainless steel sink was set into the wood. I could see faint score marks. There was a silence as he traversed the kitchen.

"You chop up bodies on that?" I asked, smiling, gesturing toward the island.

He pulled out two bottles from the fridge and twisted off the caps with a sharp hiss.

"I noticed you did that at the clinic too," he said. He pushed one of the sweating bottles into my hand. "Filling an awkward moment with a joke. Do you do that a lot?"

"I guess, yeah."

He chuckled, nudging my shoulder with the tip of his beer bottle. "Let's sit."

He led the way to a worn leather sofa, I sank into the cushions. They sighed around me. I took a long swig of the cold beer, a local craft ale. I hated beer, but I pretended to enjoy it.

"So, that…" I started, gesturing toward the sculpture with my bottle. "I'm a bit of a pleb when it comes to art and stuff. But, like, what does it mean?"

He laughed. "It's refreshing, honestly. I'm used to being around proper arty fuckers." He groaned, stretching his legs out. "I don't know how I got here. Critics and stuff. Making a living from making those is still insane to me. 'Cause I've been doing them for ages, since I was a teenager. I did them to… make sense of what I was feeling at the time. For years nobody cared, but as soon as that one blogger calls you a genius, then you're officially a genius. Makes no sense to me, but pays for all this stuff." He leaned back and rested his arm on the top of the sofa. His eyes were on the sculpture. "I mean, it's how it makes you feel. Be honest. What do you feel when you look at it? I dunno if I can even tell anymore."

My eyes traced the impossible angles and the unsettling moistness of its surface. There was a strange pull to it.

"Confused," I mumbled. Almost speaking to myself.

Jack let out a soft laugh. "Yeah. Me too." He leaned back into the sofa."Everything is confusing, isn't it? When it comes to who we are. Or who we're supposed to be. Especially as queer people." He took a slow sip of his beer. I watched the muscles in his throat work as he swallowed. "I mean, we're born with these labels, right? These Types." He took another sip. *His arms look so good under this light. Tight and vascular. I want him to grab me.* "And everyone just accepts it. Like it's perfectly normal to be defined by one thing. One talent." He gestured dismissively at his own hand. "I'm a Grip. That's a physical Type. Sticking to things. How is that supposed to..." He stopped. Laughed at himself. "Sorry. I'm talking shit."

"No," I said. "You're good."

He turned his gaze to me. "It's just. You hide it, right? If your Type isn't desirable. Or you just lie about it." His eyes held mine. "Like some people do on apps."

"Well, you're not a Grip," I shot out between sips of my beer. And even though I had just accused him, so brazenly, he just smiled. "I mean, you're not. Are you?"

"I was waiting for you to ask." His hand found my knee with a playful tap. *Please, do it again. Touch me, now.* "No. I'm not. That's just what I put on the apps. It's what I tell people." He set his bottle down on the low table between us. "It's less complicated," he added.

"Less complicated than what? What are you, then? I couldn't read you at the clinic. That's almost impossible unless someone is really, really suppressing. Or I'm drunk."

He hesitated and ran a hand through his dark hair. "It's, well, it's rare. Most people haven't even heard of it. And it doesn't fit neatly into the whole 'abilities' idea of Types." He looked at me. "My Type is Cell."

I stared at him. "Cell? I've never heard of it."

"It's a mutation. Sure you've heard of those," he continued. His voice dropped slightly. "It's about growth. Cellular growth. My touch stimulates cell and nerve regeneration in others."

He held out his hand with the palm facing up. A silent invitation. "It makes me hard to read because my energy is always changing. It depends on what I'm interacting with."

The thought of touching him was almost unbearable. My throat tightened and I knew I had to get away.

"Just a second," I mumbled. My voice was strained as I half-stood from the sofa.

I practically bolted for the bathroom, flicking on the light as I entered. A dim glow reflected off the mirror. My reflection stared back. Pale and anxious. After some deep breaths, I lifted my shirt, trailing my fingers along the faded and fresh stretch-marks tracking the skin of my stomach. I stood to the side, sucking in, then let go. *You're disgusting.*

I took a few more shaky, deep breaths, and forced myself to return. Jack was still sitting there, calm and patient.

"Hey," I started. My voice a whisper. I couldn't meet his eyes. I focused on a point just past his shoulder toward that damn statue.

"I have to tell you something. I can't have sex. Tonight. Or for a few more days."

The apology tumbled out, clumsy and juvenile. "I'm on treatment for something. I'm sorry."

I braced for the inevitable polite disappointment, the question to leave, the scoff at my assumption.

"That's fine."

I risked looking at his eyes now. His expression wasn't angry or disappointed. It was completely earnest. A small smile on his lips. "Who said anything about sex anyway?"

"You don't want to have sex?" I asked.

"I mean, I do, but… we can just talk, right? This is nice."

"Yeah. It is," I replied.

He tapped the space beside him on the couch. I joined, resting my head against the back of the couch, staring up at a rusty beam along the ceiling. After a few moments of silence, I could feel his gaze lingering on me.

"Do you ever think about your body?" He paused and seemed to choose his words carefully. "Sometimes I wish I was a Morph. Imagine just changing whenever you want to. How good would that be?" He gestured vaguely toward the sculpture. "Sometimes I think I use my statues to scratch that itch."

I looked at his face. I thought of his words from earlier. *Gorgeous*, he'd said.

"I, yeah," I managed. "I, uh, I lost a lot of weight. I thought I'd finally be happy with myself. But I just ended up with all this… uh…" My gaze lay on that beam, as if it would finish the sentence for me.

"Go ahead." He urged.

"These stretch marks and stuff." I traced an invisible line on the fabric of my shirt. "It feels like my body broke. Like I don't ever actually have control of it. Does that make sense?"

Jack listened intently.

"I know what you mean. I know it more than you think, actually." He leaned forward, his elbows rested on his knees. "My body has always been a whole thing. A constant effort to keep it contained. To stop it from changing. To stop it from affecting everything around me."

He looked at his hands. Then he looked back at me. "My Type, it's so complicated. It's why I hide it. It's why relationships are hard. Intimacy can be scary for me sometimes."

I almost scoffed. He was impossibly handsome. Lean and defined. He must have clocked my expression because his jaw tightened.

"What?"

"I mean. You're hot? What could be so difficult?" He looked hurt, genuinely hurt. And shocked. "Sorry, I just mean... Sorry."

The tension slowly eased from his shoulders. He sighed. "It's okay. It's hard to explain. When I tell people I'm self-conscious, they say the same thing."

"What does it feel like?" I whispered immediately. "Your Type. To feel it?"

He hesitated. A crease between his brows. "It's not something I just do. It's not a magic trick." He swallowed, deep, nervous. "That's what I mean about intimacy being complicated. Sex, especially, is almost impossible without a very specific kind of protection. A suit, basically. It dampens the effect. Otherwise, things can get out of hand."

"Please," my voice was suddenly fuelled with a hunger that surprised even me. "Just once. On my arm. I just want to know what it feels like."

"Kieran…" He studied me, weighing my desperation against his clear reluctance. "It's not a good idea, I'm telling you, when you feel it…"

"Please."

Something in that plea broke away his reluctance. He gave a slow nod. "*Once*. But that's it for tonight, okay? Only because you're really cute." He chuckled.

Slowly, I extended my left arm. I rested it on the space between us. His fingers were cool and soft, coming to rest on the pale of my inner forearm. Then, it began.

A low heat welling deep inside my bone. A tingling radiating from his touch. As if tiny and invisible threads were weaving patterns into my veins.

It wasn't painful, it was like scratching an overwhelmingly intense cellular itch. Liquid heat followed the tingling paths. I stared at my arm, my breath caught in my throat. I felt as though new nerves were being spun into existence, a whole new sensory network lighting up with electricity.

I gasped, snatching my arm away. The feeling vanished as soon as his fingers receded, leaving only a residual warmth. I stared at him, he smiled, waiting for me to say something. My mind was reeling.

"Please," I whispered. I held out my arm further. "Do it again."

"Kieran." Jack said.

"I don't care," He'd just shown me a key to a prison I'd been in my whole life. "Please, Jack."

He sighed. "Thought you were different."

That didn't register; it was just noise. Nothing mattered but the warmth in my forearm, the hunger. I had never been so starved. I was ravenous. Hungry for his touch.

He placed my hand in his, guiding it along with his own, to the centre of my chest. He closed his eyes. This time, the feeling was deeper, radiating heat. A sun igniting inside my ribcage. I felt a sense of expansion, as if my bones were making way for something new.

I took a breath. My lungs filled with an impossible amount of clean and full air. The relief was euphoric. I could taste the dust in the air, the metal of the fridge, everything. It was the most incredible thing I'd ever felt. And it was gone the moment he pulled his hand away again.

The loss hurt. The euphoria curdled. "More," I said.

Jack stood up from the couch. His eyes were wide. He'd seen this before. "No, Kieran. That's enough." He took a step back. "Let's catch up another time, alright?"

"No." The thought of waiting was unbearable. I lunged and grabbed his hand, clamping my fingers around his wrist.

The effect was instantaneous. A bolt of raw power shot up my arm, but this time it felt as if it were mine. The nerves in my fingertips fired into overdrive. I could feel the texture of his skin, but I could also taste it on my fingers. Salt, iron, and electricity.

"Kieran, let go!" Jack shouted. Struggling. His expression twisted from shock to genuine fear. "You don't know what you're doing!"

He was wrong. I knew exactly what I was doing.

With a strength that wasn't my own, I pulled him toward me. Wrapped my other arm around his back. Pressed my body against his. I rubbed my face against his neck. My newly sensitised skin drank in the power like I was dying of thirst.

The change began: the fabric of my shoes tore apart, the bones in my feet elongated, toes cracking down the middle with wet snaps, splitting and reforming into clawed digits. My spine unlocked; a zipper of pops shot up my back as the vertebrae multiplied. The skin along my shoulders felt too tight, so it split with a profound relief. Where my shoulders once were, now six jointed appendages punched their way out into the air, their sensitive tips quivering. My hands were then remade. My knuckles swelled into bony knobs. My fingernails peeled away from their beds like wet paper. My skull creaked, the plates shifted. A universe of information flooded my mind as my brain expanded and twisted and writhed and vibrated. I could hear the atoms dancing in the air. I could smell the thump of Jack's heart. I could feel the clamour of a tram passing three streets away.

My eyes bulged. Searing, liquid pain was washed away by ecstatic revelation as the globes split. The world fractured into a dozen perfect, overlapping images. I could see the ceiling, the floor, Jack's horrified face, and the beautiful, changing reflection of myself in the dark window, all at once.

Jack screamed as he tried to push me off him. A high, thin shriek that I could taste in the air. He finally broke free, scrambling backwards until he hit the far wall. I opened my mouth to share my joy, but my jaw tore from its hinges. It kept stretching, wider, wider, as rows of new teeth erupted from my gums in a bloody wave. My skin was no longer skin; it was a translucent membrane, secreting a clear protective mucus. It shifted from pale pink to a deep purple. I was magnificent. I'd shed the weak, soft body and become something powerful. Something no one could ever hurt or judge again.

I looked at Jack, huddled against the wall. I tried to take a step, but my original legs had fused into a single column of flesh before splitting again. They were now four long, multi-jointed limbs of exposed muscle. My new brain hadn't yet mastered them.

The world swirled with images and voices. First Paige's nails clacking. Then Gal's voice: *"More! Say it with me!"* And finally, the statue. The statue was swirling in its place like a living, breathing thing, warm and safe. I lurched forward and crashed to the floor with a heaving thud.

From my new perspective, I could see Jack. His expression shifted into something akin to sadness. The look you'd give a wombat pulverised on the side of the road. I pushed myself up. My strange new limbs dug into the wood. I stood again, taller than before, swaying as I found my balance. I flowed across the floor towards him, opening my mouth to share my joy, to beg him for the rest. What emerged from the wet mass where my mouth had once been was not a voice.

Part-song. Part-growl. A single, unmistakable, gurgled word: "MORE."

III

NO POWER BUT DEATH

no power but death

La Vecchia (The Old Woman) by Giorgione (c. 1508)

THE HOUSE HAS FALLEN QUIET, but I know it is only momentary. I am in my room, the door is locked, my back is pressed against the old wardrobe that belonged to Nanna. I have not handwritten in some time, so I do apologise if the legibility of this record may appear questionable. I retreated here when I heard the sound from down the hall, a grating of metal against stone. The sound of something coming undone. It has stopped for now, and I believe he is resting, gathering his strength. This is not an end but an intermission, a chance for me to leave this letter. It must begin where the clarity did, this morning, with the poem:

THE STICK TOGETHER FAMILIES ARE HAPPIER BY FAR,
THAN THE BROTHERS AND THE SISTERS
WHO TAKE SEPARATE HIGHWAYS ARE.
THE GLADDEST PEOPLE LIVING,
ARE THE WHOLESOME ONES WHO MAKE,
A CIRCLE AT THE FIRESIDE,
THAT NO POWER BUT DEATH CAN BREAK.

The verse surfaced alongside the milk of pre-dawn, forming in my head with immense clarity. A strange and mysterious thing, memory. Isn't it? I do not believe it is mere coincidence that I could not tell you the day of the week, nor the month, nor even the year with any confident certainty, but those words returned so whole and solid. As if they had been waiting patiently in some back room of my mind for the right moment. My mother used to recite it, among many others, while she brushed my hair before school. She loved poetry. I never quite understood it.

I have grown much older, and although wisdom is supposed to accompany age, it does very little to dull the pain I have carried. It has simply become part of an encumbering weight I am forced to bear, like a stone sewn into the lining of my coat that I have worn for so long.

When I catch my reflection in the hallway mirror, I see an elderly stranger who has stolen my eyes. An intruder in my home. Her cheeks are so hollow, in a way that makes the bones look too pointy, and her neck has grown loose and thin like a turkey's. Her clothes hang from her body in a way that would have once thrilled me, and believe me when I say I spent two decades obsessed with being smaller, counting and measuring and denying myself the simplest pleasures at the table. Such trivial, luxurious worries those seem now.

Perhaps that is the one gift this life gives in the end, the unforgiving clarity of hindsight. The way it strips away everything that does not matter and leaves you standing in the cold light of what does. But wisdom does not fill water buckets. This life is built on work.

I woke groggy, the poem already printed on my mind like fresh newsprint. Rain had hammered the roof all night, a sound I once found comforting when I was a girl, warm under my blanket. These days it is just a catalogue of anxieties, for every gurgle is another reminder to check the barrels, and every shudder a warning of a new leak in the roof that I will have to patch. The true fear delivered by the storm was the one that had me holding my breath with every roll of thunder, straining for any stir from Joseph's room down the hall. My husband's sleep had grown terribly fragile you see, and the slightest disturbance could set him off into one of his states.

When the rain finally calmed to a gentle patter and then to silence, I listened to the stillness from his room and felt a small relief. Nothing from Harry's room either, which was not unusual, for he has always been a deep sleeper. I paused at his doorway on my way to the kitchen, a morning ritual that I have maintained since the early days when everything changed. The door was closed, as it always is now, and I pressed my palm flat against the wood.

"Harry?" I whispered, but he did not stir, and I heard no movement from within. I told myself he was simply tired, that teenagers need their sleep, that he would be hungry when he finally woke. I would have something warm and nourishing waiting for him. I would check on him properly after I had seen to the animals and the water and all the other tasks that this day demands.

In the kitchen, I filled the kettle from the barrel by the front door and set it on the stove, a flame of which I had to coerce back to life with meagre kindling and a plethora of patience. While I waited for the water to heat, I stood at the window and watched the light over the paddocks, the dead grass still wet from the rain, the treeline at the far boundary dark and dripping.

Before I allowed myself the first sip of tea, the small ritual of pleasure that I have guarded jealously through all of this, I went to my husband. I slipped into Joseph's room, where the air was heavy with his particular scent. The curtains were drawn and the darkness was nearly complete, but I could make out the shape of him on the bed, the bulk of his body motionless beneath the heavy blankets. I crossed to him carefully, avoiding the floorboard near the dresser that creaked, and bent to give him a quick kiss on his cool, dry forehead. His skin felt papery under my lips, and he did not respond to my touch, but I whispered good morning to him anyway and told him I would bring him something to eat later.

Stepping outside afterwards, basket hanging from my elbow, the cold was a violent ambush. The air found every flaw in my amateur jumper, a word I use loosely, for it is more a collection of patchy wool stuck together crudely with twine. My sister Mary was the real knitter in our family, producing cardigans and scarves and intricate blankets that people actually wanted to use. She learned from our Pop, his rough hands patient over hers, guiding the needles through the yarn while she sat on his knee. I have only a faint memory of watching them together by the fire.

I pulled the wool tighter around myself and began the walk to the barn, my boots leaving deep, crunching prints in the frost that coated the grass. My breath came out in white clouds that hung in the still air before dissolving. When I reached the barn, the big door resisted, its dampened wood swollen tight in the frame. I put my shoulder into it, feeling the ache spread across my back. It groaned open reluctantly, releasing a rush of warm air.

Inside, the air was sweet; manure that needed mucking out, hay, and the living scent of fur and feather that tends to radiate from an animal's body. Marlena, my eldest cow, turned her burly head at my entrance, her dark eyes watching me with that patient gaze. Gorgeous girl. I crossed to her and ran my hand along her spine, feeling the knobs of her vertebrae, far more prominent beneath my palm than they had been even a month ago. She needed better feed, more grain, the kind of care I am not certain I can provide much longer. "Morning, girl," I whispered, leaning my forehead against hers. "Another day. We keep going though, hm?"

After the cows, the chickens. The coop was damp and the hens were irritable, fluffing their feathers and muttering their complaints as I reached beneath them for the eggs. I collected five, a good day, each one warm in my palm before I nestled them carefully into my basket. I allowed myself to feel satisfaction, for five eggs meant protein, meant another day of strength, meant that I could keep this small household fed a little longer.

Hauling the rainwater back to the house, my next task, was torture of the most necessary kind. The wire handles of the buckets always bit into my palms, leaving red marks, and my back screamed in bloody murder every step. I am not young anymore, though I cannot say exactly how old I am now. Time has become slippery and strange in a way it never was before. I set the buckets down on the front porch and stood for a moment with my hands on my hips. I paused, breathing the stinging cold air, looking out at the land.

After I had caught my breath, I poured the buckets into the large water barrels, then began the perimeter walk. The fence surrounding our property was not so much built as accumulated; a weary line of scavenged wire and rusted panels. It would not stop anything truly determined, I knew that, but checking it had become a comfort I could not afford to abandon, a ritual of sorts. I walked the line slowly, testing the tension of the wire, looking for gaps or weaknesses, my eyes constantly scanning the treeline and the road and the distant shapes of neighbouring properties.

My gaze drifted, as it often does, to the Moore place on the nearby acreage. It had been silent for weeks now, the windows dark. And there was no smoke from the chimney in ages, no movement in the yard where Jim's dog used to run in circles barking.

The memory of my last walk over there stops me from ever trying again. It sits in my chest like a cold bucket of water whenever I think of it. The silence had hit me first that day. All the usual noises that had drifted down from their property for as long as I could remember were simply gone: Jim shouting, the rumble of his tractor, even Linda's voice calling the kids in after dark. I had told myself they might have gone to town, or maybe they left to find family elsewhere, but something in my gut knew better even then. On their verandah, Linda's famed pot plants were brown and dead, hundreds of them.

I had forced myself to approach the front door, my heart beating so hard it almost knocked me over. I tapped on the door, once, twice, three times. The sound was swallowed by the house, absorbed into whatever waited inside. I called out Linda's name, then Jim's. Only the wind and creaks answered, stirring the dead leaves that had gathered on the porch. I did not try the handle. I could not make myself do it, could not bear to know what I would find if the door swung open.

As I turned to leave, I glanced up at their bedroom window on the second floor. For a second, I saw it, or thought I saw it: the shape of a face, a shadow standing behind the glass. Or perhaps it was only a curtain moving, or a trick of the light, or my own fear playing tricks on me. I did not stay to find out. I fled, stumbling down their driveway, every snap of a twig behind me sounding like a footstep. I did not look back until the lock on my own door was turned and I was standing in my own kitchen with my back against the wall. I never went back.

I opened the chest freezer that sits in the corner where the book cabinet used to stand. The frozen air smelled so metallic. We were running low, I could see that immediately, the white parts of the freezer more visible than it should be, the remaining packages fewer than I had hoped. I pulled out a frozen parcel wrapped in old fabric from shredded clothes, and I set it on the counter while I prepared the vegetables.

I decided on a stew, the kind of simple meal we used to make on winter Sundays, the pot simmering on the stove for hours. As I chopped the hard carrots, and the potatoes that had begun to sprout white eyes, the knife slipped and caught the side of my finger. A sharp sting, and then I watched, completely mesmerised as a perfect bead of blood welled up from the puncture. I put my finger in my mouth, tasting copper, and thought of nothing at all. What a strange relief, I thought.

The stew's richness filled the house as it cooked, and I allowed myself to breathe it in deeply, soothing me. When it was ready, I ladled out a bowl and carried it carefully down the hall to Harry's room.

I knocked softly on his door, the same door I had stood outside this morning, and called his name in my most gentle voice. "Harry, love, I've brought you something to eat. You must be hungry by now." There was no response, only a faint sound, a kind of shuffling or stirring that might have been bedclothes adjusting. I balanced the bowl in one hand and reached for my keys with the other, the jingle heavy with all the locks this house requires.

I unlocked the door and pushed it open with my hip. The curtains were drawn against the daylight and Harry was on his bed, or rather, on the mattress I had moved to the floor for safety. He was thrashing against the chains on his wrists that secured him to the anchor point I had installed in the wall. His eyes, when he turned to look at me, were a milky white, and there was nothing in them that recognised me, nothing of the boy who had once run into my arms.

"Shhh, Harry, it's alright," I soothed, keeping my voice calm and steady, the way I speak to Marlena when she is startled. "Mum's here. I've brought you something nice. Stew, look."

I set the bowl down by his side and stepped back quickly, for I have learned to be careful, to respect the unpredictability. It used to be dangerous to feed him, before I took the pliers to his teeth. He kept biting, you see, not just at me but at himself, his tongue nearly severed more than once during his fits, the blood pouring from his mouth until I thought he would drown in it. Worse though, his confusion frightened me. He would often mistake his own arm for a meal and had taken large chunks from it with his own teeth. I had caught him one morning, gnawing on what was left of his hand. So, taking the teeth was a mercy, really, a practical solution, and I do not regret it even though the sound of them coming loose still makes me feel sick.

When he was calmer, the meat having its usual sluggish effect, I settled into the chair I kept by the door and read to him from a children's book I found in the library in town. Its pages were water-stained but still very much legible. I do not know if he understands the words anymore, if anything of my son remains inside the body that used to hold him, but I read anyway because it is what mothers do.

For a breathtaking second, as I reached the end of a verse, he seemed to lean into my touch when I reached out to stroke his hair, a ghost of the boy he was surfacing through whatever darkness had claimed him.

Then he snapped, his jaws closing on empty air where my hand had been a fraction of a second before. His gums snapped together with a sort of wet clap. I pulled back so fast I nearly fell.

I was barely out of his room, turned the key in the lock, when the loud crash came from down the hall. Joseph. My stomach dropped and I hurried toward his door. When I pressed my ear to the wood, I could hear him moving inside, the clink of chain links rattling against each other.

I turned the key and opened the door just a crack, just enough to see inside, and he lunged, his body slamming against the door with a force that knocked me backward. The chain snapped taut, jerking him back, and I heard the bolt in the stone floor groan under the strain. I caught a glimpse of his face, and there was nothing left. Nothing of the man I had married in the small ceremony I conducted myself in the living room, nothing of the tenderness I had imagined in his eyes when I first brought him home. Only hunger.

He had found me, you know, the same way I found Harry. On the road from town, a stumbling shadow against the sun, moving with that terrible lurch that I have learned to recognise from a great distance. Others might have seen a monster, might have run or reached for a weapon. I saw a man in need of a home, a lost soul who deserved a chance at the kind of life I was building here. I saw my grandfather's hands in the way his fingers curled. So I gave him that same name, called him Joseph and spoke to him gently as I led him back to the house. I installed him in what used to be my sister Ellie's room before she left, before they all left. I secured him with chains I had salvaged from an abandoned hardware store.

I left his portion of meat just inside the doorway, sliding it across the floor with my foot so I would not have to reach within his range, and I retreated quickly. But not before I saw that the bolt anchoring his chain to the floor was coming loose, the stone around it cracked and crumbled from the constant strain of his pulling. It was then that the grating sound began, the metal-on-stone sound that sent me scurrying to my room to write his account while I still can.

***

The grating has started again. Louder now. More insistent. My pencil freezes on the page and I sit very still, listening. Metal on stone, a grinding, patient sound. It stops. The silence that follows is worse.

Most people would have run when things began to change. My sisters certainly did. Sarah went north, chasing rumours of a safe zone that probably never existed. Ellie went east, toward the coast, convinced that the oceans would have answers. Mary simply disappeared one night, leaving nothing but a note that said she was sorry and she loved me and she could not stay. They knew the feeling of being abandoned, Dad had left us the same way, driving off one morning and never coming back, yet they inflicted that same wound on me without a second thought. So I made my own family. My husband. My son. My circle at the fireside.

A tremendous crash echoes from down the hall, and I feel it through the floor, through the walls, through my entire body. It is the definite sound of splintering wood and tortured metal finally giving way to relentless pressure. He is out. My breath catches and I set down my pencil, my hand trembling. I hear a heavy, dragging step in the hallway, large and clumsy as it finds its footing. Then another step, closer. He is coming.

I find that I am not afraid. He is my husband. I chose him, named him, made him mine through the simple act of refusing to give up on him. When he comes through that door, it will not be an act of violence, no. It will be an embrace, the final closing of a circle that I have spent my whole life trying to complete. I think of Mum fixing my hair, of my grandfather's patient hands, of the sisters who left me and the family I built from what remained.

The footsteps stop. Right outside my door. I can hear his breathing now, wet and laboured, and I picture him standing there in the dark of the hallway, his head tilted, listening for me.

A low scratching begins, a fingernail dragging down the wood, and I close my eyes.

The scratching stops. Now he is banging, he is kicking. The old wood of my bedroom door shudders with each impact, groaning against the hinges that have held firm for a hundred years but were never meant for this. It will not hold much longer.

The stick-together families are happier by far. I will now rise from my chair and walk toward the door. I will be with my husband.

IV

SANCTUARY

sanctuary

Christ at the Column by Antonello da Messina (c. 1476)

THE AD CAUGHT DANIEL AT ONE IN THE MORNING, when he couldn't tell if the ringing in his ears was tinnitus or the mini fridge's compressor. He was reading a forum thread about some SNES game he'd never actually finished, just looked at screenshots of, when the browser went dark. His reflection appeared on the monitor. Then the silhouette, pulsing:

"Do you seek true connection?" The voice said.

A woman's face rendered in pixel-perfect clarity faded up from black. Then her body, as the camera pulled out. She was naked. It cut to fingers on a spine, then lips smacking together, then a tear rolling down a cheek that looked like it had been buffed with a microfibre cloth.

"*The Veil*. True connection," the woman whispered.

His reflection again. He looked like his dad. Everyone said that. He hated it. He was thirty-four. He still had the same body he'd had at fifteen: the soft middle that wouldn't harden no matter what he did, the shoulders that slumped like an old oak. His father had made him do push-ups in the garage every morning for a whole summer holiday. It hadn't changed anything.

The suit was in the corner, plugged in. The charging light made the room look like the inside of an aquarium, but more purple than blue. He'd bought it three months ago, the day after a really awful coffee date where he'd excused himself to the bathroom and then just left. Just walked out the back entrance. He could still feel his shirt sticking to his sweaty back, the way his hands had been shaking so badly he'd dropped his car keys twice in the car park.

The forums said everyone used THE VEIL to fuck. Daniel hadn't. He'd done the 'Glimpses' a few times, the little preview windows where you talked to someone for five minutes before deciding if you wanted more. But he always logged out before anything happened. Last week, though, he'd ordered the upgrade. The full experience, they called it. The genital nodes. They'd come in a black padded envelope with no return address, and when he'd opened it, he felt nauseous, shoving them deep in a drawer somewhere. The thought made his face hot even now, alone, at one in the morning.

He got up and pulled the suit off the charger. It smelled like the inside of a new car, but also sweat. The material was thin and sticky against his fingers. It had cooled down from charging but it still felt wrong. Like touching something that had recently been alive.

He stripped to his undies and stepped into it. The mesh pulled at his leg hair. The nodes clicked against his wrists, his temples, his knees, his ankles, his feet, his shoulder, his chest, his stomach. The adhesive ones for his thighs went on easily. Then the others. His hands shook. The two small pads for his genitals had a different texture, tacky but not sticky, as if to protect from any unwanted waxing. When he pressed them onto his balls, shaft, and taint, there was a vibration. Brief. Like a phone notification from inside his cock. He thought about confession. Of all things. He thought about the pamphlet his father had left on his bed when he was sixteen, the one with the silhouette of a man at the edge of a dark forest and the words FINDING YOUR STRENGTH: RETURNING TO GOD in big letters. Did he still have that pamphlet? Maybe he could read it now. Maybe it was important, maybe it would help him.

The headset part of the suit was scuffed along one edge where he'd dropped it a few times. It pressed against his cheeks. When he put it on, his own breath came back at him, stale. He always started sweating when he put it on, but he liked the feeling.

The login screen was far too bright, he'd shut his eyes until the white faded. Then the manufactured smell hit him, a gentle spray from the middle section of the headset. It was supposed to be mint, but it smelt more like that foamy shit you're forced to hold in your mouth at the dentist. He breathed it in anyway. It was supposed to clear your senses and prepare you for the world you were about to enter.

He closed his eyes and let the loading sequence take him.

The plaza, when it loaded, was circular and full of noise. Not real noise, it just felt like standing near an electrical substation. Lots of buzzing and a strong feeling of electricity in the air. Avatars blinked into existence around him. A woman with wings made of rainbow. A chrome robot with enormous biceps. Someone who looked exactly like a default character, probably a first-timer.

Daniel's avatar loaded around him. Lia. She had heavy blonde hair and a black dress. When he looked down at her body, his body, there was always a lag, a fraction of a second where the hands moved after he moved them. Her waist was narrow, but she had shape to her. Her chest was full.

Sometimes Daniel caught himself walking differently as Lia. Shoulders back, chin up.

A mirror floated in front of him. He looked at her face.

"Hey wanna sync-fuck? Full haptics now no chat just fun."

The voice message appeared next to a red avatar with enormous muscles. MAXPOW, the name said, as he revealed himself from behind the mirror.

"No thanks."

MAXPOW disappeared.

"Query: Desired interaction parameters. Please input preferred duration, haptic intensity level, and primary arousal vector."

This one was chrome-plated, voice flat.

"I'm okay."

Gone.

There were others. A squirrel with human eyes talking too fast about the new nodes. An avatar with breasts so large they clipped through her torso when she turned.

"Hey honey. Glimpse?"

Lia walked past. Daniel walked past. He was about to log out when he saw the guy standing alone near one of the portal entrances.

The avatar was simple. Dark hair, white t-shirt, clean black slacks. He wasn't moving much. He was watching the chaos like someone at a party they hadn't wanted to come to. His nametag said ADAM.

Lia sent the Glimpse request before Daniel could talk her out of it. Adam turned. His face wasn't handsome in the overdone way most male avatars were. He just looked like a person.

"Evening."

"Hi."

A pause. The winged woman laughed, the rainbow glowing more intensely along with the bellow.

"Trying to avoid the, uh." Adam gestured at the chaos. "Whatever this is."

"Yeah."

"It's a lot."

"It is."

Lia could feel her real body sweating under the mesh.

"You seem, I don't know." Adam scratched his cheek. "Different? That sounds like a line. Sorry. I just mean you're not, you know."

"Not what?"

"Not trying to get me to do something in the first thirty seconds."

Lia smiled.

"Was that a real scratch?" she asked.

"Hm?"

"What you just did, when you asked me the question. You said, 'you seem, I don't know', and then you scratched your cheek. Was that because your cheek was itchy, or was it a sort of social tic?"

"You're interesting." He said with a smile. "What brings you here?"

"I'm really not sure."

"Me either."

The pair watched the hoards of avatars rushing by, pointing every now and then at particularly grotesque and/or colourful ones.

"Are you a good listener?" Lia asked, just like that.

"I try. Yeah. I talk too much when I'm nervous. Which is most of the time."

They talked for a while longer. About how strange the plaza was, how most people seemed to be here for one thing and one thing only (to fuck). Adam kept stopping mid-sentence, restarting, like he was editing himself. It was clumsy. Lia liked it; so did Daniel.

When Lia sent the Affirm request, her hand was shaking.

Adam affirmed.

The beach loaded slowly, and in chunks. The internet needed an upgrade; Daniel would look into it soon. First the sky; a pinkish colour with two moons that looked like they'd been copy-pasted side-by-side. Then the sand, fine and completely uniform. Then the sound of waves, which was clear and beautiful. Better than the plaza noise.

Adam was standing in front of her. The moonlight made his white shirt look pink.

"Nice, isn't it?"

"Yeah."

They walked along the shore, not speaking at all. THE VEIL had a way of making those moments feel far less necessary to be filled by trivial conversation. Namely due to the beauty of the digital landscape serving as a distraction, how realistically beautiful it felt, but there was something about the anonymity that allowed Daniel to feel completely at ease. Even with this complete stranger, she felt as if he could be comfortable in silence, something he would immediately have read as rejection in the unforgiving landscape of real life.

"Sorry." Adam eventually said as they reached a large collection of rocks, the waves crashing against them.

"What for?"

"I said I talk a lot when I'm nervous, but I'm not talking at all."

"Means you're comfortable I guess. Me too."

As they reached some rocks, they realised they weren't the texture of rock at all. They were black glass, the kind of geological feature that only existed in virtual worlds. Along the glassy surface lay bright, glowing blue moss. They sat.

Adam's hand touched her chin. The node on Daniel's cheek fired, a warm pressure, gentle. It felt like being touched. It felt real.

"You're beautiful," Adam said. Then, quieter: "Can I kiss you?"

Lia's throat closed. He thought about the pamphlet again. The dark edge of the forest. The way her father had never mentioned it, just left it there like a threat made out of paper.

"Yes."

The kiss was data. Daniel knew that. But the nodes translated it into warmth and pressure. The scent spray on the helmet emanated a warm mist, like hot breath, on Daniel's mouth. Adam's hands moved to her back, his waist. The new nodes activated, a spreading heat that made Daniel's real body arch off the bed he now lay on.

Strangely, he thought about being seven years old and finding a wasp nest in the backyard. It was dead, if that was possible, fallen from somewhere up high and drying in the sun. He wanted to touch the dead wasp nest, but felt like he couldn't touch it, out of some sort of pre-determined fear. If he touched it, he'd get in trouble, or he'd get stung, or both, even though it was dry and dead and not a wasp in sight. He didn't know why that memory came now.

They were on the moss. Adam was above her. The suit translated weight, pressure, the simulation of breath against her neck. Lia was crying but she didn't know it yet. The tears were collecting in the foam padding of the headset.

Adam slid a finger from Lia's knee, to her thigh, to her underwear, pulling them down slowly, so slowly. The same finger trailed the same path, now finding her pussy, wet and throbbing. Adam paused there.

"Please." She whined through a whisper. "Please."

He pushed, and he tickled, and he twisted his fingers up and down and in and out. Daniel felt it, all of it. The nodes firing through his crotch, his own hand rubbing the hardness pushing through the suit.

When Lia came, it wasn't like anything she had felt before. It was good and it was awful and it felt like falling. The nodes along her groin vibrated and moved and pulsed and danced. She was wet, a mess. But she loved it. He lay there, on his bed, on the moss, her moss, staring up into the digital sky above them. The waves looped. The moons didn't move.

"You know," Adam said, "my old man used to say, 'No rest for the wicked, and not much for the righteous either.' Used to say it whenever I tried to have a kip on the lounge.

Drove me mental." He laughed, dry. "But here, we can just... stay. No rush."

Daniel's body went cold. Lia shuddered, freezing on the spot.

The nodes on his genitals suddenly felt like burns. Like hot metal on his skin. Daniel could feel vomit rising in his throat. Actual vomit, in his real body, in his real bedroom.

Lia scrambled backwards. The movement was jerky, the avatar lagging behind the panic.

"Lia? What's wrong?"

"I have to go."

"What? Why? Did I do something?"

Adam's face. Adam's eyes. Lia looked at them, really looked at them this time.

"I have to go."

He found the emergency logout button. His real fingers were shaking so hard it took three tries as he fumbled.

Black. Total black. Then his bedroom. The ceiling with the water stain, maybe black mould, he didn't care. The smell of his own sweat. The smell of his cum.

Daniel lay there. He couldn't move. The suit was sticking to him everywhere, the nodes cooling rapidly, leaving wet patches where they'd been warm. His genitals felt like they belonged to someone else. He thought about cutting them off. The thought was clear and specific and he was almost certain he didn't mean it. But maybe he could.

He pulled the headset off. His face was wet. He was still crying.

He lay there until the light through his curtains turned grey.

***

Sunday came with church bells tolling from down the road. He hadn't slept. The suit was in the corner, a shed snake skin. An evil serpent he had destroyed. He had spent the last two hours in the shower, his skin red raw.

His phone buzzed. *Running 10 mins late. Put the kettle on.*

He didn't put the kettle on. He showered again. The water was too hot and he didn't adjust it. His skin turned red, redder. He got dressed in clothes that didn't match.

His father was on the doorstep. Arthur Coleman. Grey hair, straight posture, mole next to his right eye, thin lips.

"You were up all night again playing your games? I can always tell."

The car smelled like the same fucking freshener his father had used in there for fifteen years. The same one. Daniel stared out the window.

Church was bad. Really, really bad. The saints on the stained glass seemed to lean toward him, like they wanted to pull out his hair. The pew was harder and narrower than it ever had been. He couldn't sit still. During the sermon, his father's voice boomed about the wages of a corrupt heart, and Daniel thought about the beach, the pink sand, the way Adam's hand had felt inside her.

When it was over, another hand landed on his shoulder. "Daniel. A word." His father said, stern, cold.

The study by the entrance was small; just a desk, books, bibles, books, more bibles and two chairs. Jesus hung behind his father, crying, staring up into nothing.

"You seem troubled." Arthur cleared his throat. Don't you do that before you speak?

"I'm fine."

"You're not." Arthur was using his quiet voice. "The confessional is always open."

Daniel said nothing.

"Secrets weigh heavily. Especially the ones we keep from ourselves. The unnatural ones. The ones that fester." Arthur said.

Daniel's throat had closed. He couldn't swallow. He thought about Lia's throat, which was long and elegant and nothing like his own.

"I've seen it for years, Daniel. I prayed I was wrong. But I see it. It's a sickness. A perversion. God offers forgiveness. But first you must confess. You must name it."

His father was now standing between him and the door. Daniel thought about the dress he wore that one time. He took it from his aunt, stuffed it into his bag after school. He'd been about fifteen. His father had never said a word. Just left that pamphlet. The dark forest. *FINDING YOUR STRENGTH: RETURNING TO GOD.* Something shifted in Daniel's chest. Not courage.

"You're right, Dad," he said. His voice sounded like someone else's. "Maybe it is time."

FINDING YOUR STRENGTH: RETURNING TO GOD.

The confessional was at the back of the church. The wood was black with age and oil from hands. The brass handle was cold.

Inside, the kneeler was worn velvet. It bit into his knees.
FINDING YOUR STRENGTH: RETURNING TO GOD.

Through the grille, a shadow. The shape of his father, waiting.

"Bless me, Father, for I have sinned. It's been… a while since my last confession."

Arthur cleared his throat. He did it right this time.

"Speak, my son."
FINDING YOUR STRENGTH.

Daniel breathed in. The air was thin.

"Do you remember, father, when I was a kid. There was a wasp nest in the backyard. It was dead, like, dried up. Completely dried up. The sun had done its thing. I was so scared of it. Terrified. There was nothing to sting me, the nest was dead and empty, but I was so scared." Daniel felt tears trying to push themselves out, he swallowed them back. "My Dad. He was the one… the one who made me scared. Terrified. Of nothing. No danger. I tried on a dress… just one time, when I was a teenager. And it felt so right, Dad. And you made me so fucking scared."

"This isn't really—" Arthur muttered.

"Listen to me. Shut up. Shut up and listen to me." Daniel interrupted. He thought about the beach. The moons. The way Adam had said "a little kip on the lounge" and the way his voice had slipped into that comfortable tone, the one Daniel had heard his whole life.

He leaned closer to the grille. His lips almost touching the wood.

FINDING YOUR STRENGTH.

"My username," he said, "is Lia."

Silence.

"Dad."

The sound from the other side was a strangled mess, like someone trying to breathe after being shot. Daniel waited. He could feel his own pulse in his ears. It almost hurt, but it felt so good. He could feel the node points on his body, phantom sensations, even though the dead skin was back in his apartment. He leaned closer. "Hard to get any rest, isn't it?" His voice was barely even a whisper. "Wicked or righteous." He paused. He let it sting. "Especially after a long night of games. Adam." Nothing from the other side. Just breathing. Daniel stayed on his knees. He closed his eyes. For thirty-four years he'd been told he was the thing that was wrong. The aberration. The sickness. Now he knew which of them it actually was.

"I am so sorry. I am so, so sorry." A crying mess of a noise from the other side. "You know I love you. You know I care. I am so sorry. I don't… I don't know what to say." Sobbing.

"I forgive you. I do." Calm.

White screen.

THANK YOU FOR USING THE VEIL. IF YOU ENJOYED THIS EXPERIENCE, PLEASE CONSIDER LEAVING A REVIEW. IF YOU WOULD LIKE TO UPGRADE YOUR EXPERIENCE, PLEASE VISIT OUR WEBSITE TO PURCHASE FURTHER EXPLORATION HOURS. THANK YOU FOR USING THE VEIL.

V

CORNERS

corners

The Mocking of Christ by Fra Angelico (c. 1440)

[Friday, 12 Jul, 9:38 PM] **Jess:** OMG. LiaM. Best date ever.

[Friday, 12 Jul, 9:38 PM] **Jess:** He is literally perfect aahhh!!!! Is it too soon to say I'm in love? LOL.

[Friday, 12 Jul, 9:39 PM] **Liam:** YAS JESS! Get itttt! Seeeeeee?
Told you it was a good vibe to get tinder and try dating again!!! So is he hot irl? Cus his profile pic was a bit dry lol?

[Friday,12 Jul, 9:41 PM] **Jess:** hes... a bit intense. In a good way.
Dark hair nd dark eyes. Honestly sooo hot tho. He was talking about some really weird stuff ?? ngl...

[Friday, 12 Jul, 9:41 PM] **Jess:** Like he was going on about... like geometry, like shapes ? Idk I might be too many wines to get it haha. But he's cool.... Im peeing lmao.

[Friday, 12 Jul, 9:42 PM] **Jess:** But he is not nt boring!! For once I got a date and he isnt so boring. He doesn't have a phone tho, is that red flag? LMAO...

[Friday, 12 Jul, 9:46 PM] **Liam:** Geometry?? Sure why not, and no phone? lol. I mean, it can be kinda cool... u could digital detox together, lol. but no phone feels so rare...? Ok but I also NEED photo pls!!!

[Friday, 12 Jul, 9:47 PM] **Jess:** Fine, fine. But he really hates photos he said. I have to be sneaky one sec.

[Friday, 12 Jul, 9:47 PM] **Jess: [IMAGE]**

[Friday, 12 Jul, 9:52 PM] **Jess:** Don't leave me hanging lol, do u think he's hot or am i drunk

[Friday, 12 Jul, 9:53 PM] **Liam:** Jess.

[Friday, 12 Jul, 9:54 PM] **Liam:** Who ... what the fuck.

[Friday, 12 Jul, 9:54 PM] **Liam:** I'm not being funny, I'm not joking. Who the fuck is that man. Zoom in on his face. Look at his face in person? Can you not see what I'm seeing? My blood just went so cold. Get away from him. Now. Please.

[Friday, 12 Jul, 9:55 PM] **Jess:** Wtf? See what? Ur not funny lol. We're about to go back to his. Talk soon

[Friday, 12 Jul, 9:56 PM] **Liam:** JESS DO NOT GO TO HIS HOUSE. I AM BEGGING YOU. THERE IS SOMETHING WRONGg WITH THAAT PHOTO. Send me ur location NOW

[Friday, 12 Jul, 9:57 PM] **Jess:** WTF relax! Why r u being like this??? The photo is a bit blurry .... I don't want to be rude hes fully waiting for me.... Will send pin dw

[Friday, 12 Jul, 10:19 PM] **Jess:** [LOCATION PIN]

[Friday, 12 Jul, 10:20 PM] **Liam:** Jess that pin isn't even, ? It's like... a lake and a random road??? Fuck. Just be safe please.
[Friday, 12 Jul, 10:28PM] **Liam:** Checkin in, are you all good?????

[Friday, 12 Jul, 10:34 PM] **Liam:** Legit just watching my phone waiting for u to reply....????

[Friday, 12 Jul, 10:39PM] **Liam:** answer ur phone please..... I have such a bad feeling please answer

[Friday, 12 Jul, 10:40PM] **Liam:** jess answer.... Ffs....

[Friday, 12 Jul, 10:51PM] **Liam:** ok i dont want u to freak out if u see this but i am gonna call police soon if u dont reply, i just have this weird feeling in my gut i can feel something is wrong jess.

[Friday, 12 Jul, 11:20PM] **Liam:** i called police but they said to just keep them updated so please reply ASAP or i will send them that location and they will be there please jess, wtf is going on....

[Friday, 12 Jul, 11:46 PM] **Jess:** His house Liam. I am at his house now, and t the waalls. The floors amd floora. No furniture noint nothing no he

[Friday, 12 Jul, 11:46 PM] **Jess:** Ahl

[Friday, 12 Jul, 11:47 PM] **Jess:** hepl

[Friday, 12 Jul, 11:47 PM] **Jess:** n o winows bhave to bfn uq eiet
[Friday, 12 Jul, 11:48 PM] **Liam:** THANK FUCK ANSWER UR PHONE POLEASE

[Friday, 12 Jul, 11:49 PM] **Jess:** im in t bathroom. liam scared

[Friday, 12 Jul, 11:50 PM] **Liam:** jess just L:EAVE PLEASE! WHAT IS

[Friday, 12 Jul, 11:50 PM] **Liam:** GOING ON!!!

[Friday, 12 Jul, 11:51 PM] **Jess:** fuck

[Friday, 12 Jul, 11:52 PM] **Liam:** please answer ur phone

[Friday, 12 Jul, 11:58 PM] **Liam:** calling ur mum

[Friday, 12 Jul, 12:09 AM] **Liam:** pleaser jess answer

[Saturday, 13 Jul, 12:30 AM] **Liam:** she's on her way to mine. We're calling the policetogether . Plea tell me where u are

[Saturday, 13 Jul, 1:16 AM] **Jess:** Liam need to be fast

[Saturday, 13 Jul, 1:17 AM] **Jess:** He took me into a room

[Saturday, 13 Jul, 1:17 AM] **Liam:** IV$ CALLED U ONE HUNDRED TIMES UJR MUM is here

[Saturday, 13 Jul, 1:18 AM] **Jess:** Listen to me.

[Saturday, 13 Jul, 1:19 AM] **Jess:** He took me into the room. It wasn't really a room. Think of, static, on a TV. Inside that. Right in. Keep going. There. We're here. Listen to me, Liam. He showed me. The room, all of it, how it's inside our bodies, inside our heads. It was so fucking beautiful Liam. He was dancing. But, how he really is, not what I thought he was. He is so beautiful, Liam. He took my eyes. Listen now, Liam, listen to me. Please. Listen. Can you hear me? Where you are? I am calling you, so loud. Can you hear me?

[Saturday, 13 Jul, 1:20 AM] **Liam:** what the fuck are you saying jess. the police are here with ius now. they are tracking your phone. PLEASE.

[Saturday, 13 Jul, 1:21 AM] **Jess:** Driving

[Saturday, 13 Jul, 1:22 AM] **Jess:** Niam is driving me somewhere. I am blind now. There is a lot of blood where my eyes were.

[Saturday, 13 Jul, 1:23 AM] **Liam:** DRIVING YOU WHERE JESS? SEND PIN. GIVE ME A STREET SIG OR SOMETHING ICAN COME NOW

[Saturday, 13 Jul, 1:45 AM] **Jess:** OMG. LiaM. Best date ever.

[Saturday, 13 Jul, 1:46 AM] **Liam:** ....

[Saturday, 13 Jul, 1:47 AM] **Jess:** ?? I'm with Niam. The Tinder datE?? He's amazing! Legit so hot lol...

[Saturday, 13 Jul, 1:47 AM] **Liam:** JESS STOP IT. THIS ISN'T FUNNY. LOOK AT YOUR TEXT HISTORY. YOU WERE JUST AT HIS HOUSE. R You fucking KIDDING me?

[Saturday, 13 Jul, 1:48 AM] **Jess:** wtf.... I'm at pub with him now??. Chill? e wants to show me his house, do i go? Lol

[Saturday, 13 Jul, 1:48 AM] **Liam:** NO. JESS. DON'T GO.

[Saturday, 13 Jul, 2:30 AM] **Liam:** Jess

[Saturday, 13 Jul, 3:15 AM] **Liam:** Please answer me.

[Saturday, 13 Jul, 9:15 AM] **Liam:** The police are going to the pin from last night. I'm so scared Jess. Please just be okay.

[Saturday, 13 Jul, 1:00 PM] **Liam:** The police said there was heaps of blood there.... Where r you... i miss u... and i just know... i fucking know ur dead i can feel it.

[Sunday, 14 Jul, 6:20 PM] **Liam:** They asked about Niam today and couldn't give them a last name. The photo.... U sent me, Jess... it's fucking gone? from our chat... no record of it. They think Im lying... I even took a screenshot i sent it to Jace when it all happened but it's just a blank screen. he even said it was always just a black box.... No pic.... I remember it so clearly tho...

[Tuesday, 23 Jul, 11:03 AM] **Liam:** It's like u just evaporated. ur poor parents. we're all... it's like we're all dead Jess

[Friday, 16 Aug, 10:55 PM] **Liam:** Hey Jess. It's been a month. Feels like everything is so different now. I keep re-reading this chat. Trying to make sense of anything at all.... Nothing makes sense.

[Friday, 16 Aug, 10:56 PM] **Liam:** I feel like I'm going insane keeping it all in. No one believes me. I'm losing my mind. I swear I saw the pic

[Friday, 16 Aug, 10:57 PM] **Liam:** It was his fucking eyes, Jess. He didn't have any EYES. It was BLACK JUST BLACK. Ttwo holes,, Two perfect, dark holes.... And he was just smiling at me like he could see thru the fucking phone and wanted tohurt me... it was so clear and the feeling was so intense.... Cnt get it out of my fiucking head... just smiling at looking at me, not at the camera, at me

[Friday, 16 Aug, 10:58 PM] **Liam:** I should stop now, texting u. ut Im terrified of forgetting everything and i dont want to give up on u.... But ....i'm not sure...

[Saturday, 17 Aug, 9:15 PM] **Liam:** he is in my dreams.... U too... i have to stop... i cant sleep anymore and i think im going crazy

[Friday, 28th Aug, 11:00 PM] **Liam:** I miss you..

[Saturday, 19th December, 3:01 AM] **Jess:** OMG. LiaM. Best date ever.

[Saturday, 19th December, 3:02 AM] **Jess:** hes so hot....
[Saturday, 19th December, 3:03 AM] **Jess:** **[IMAGE]**

VI

LIKE A BIRD'S WING

like a bird's wing

The Head of Medusa by Peter Paul Rubens (c. 1618)

EVERY MORNING, FOR JAVIER, started with the same grim calculation of his existence: what part of himself was he willing to auction off just to keep breathing for another twenty-four hours? It was a constant, exhausting accounting. In the rare moments when the city loosened its grip, Javier would allow himself to remember. Remember a time before his accounting began. A different life.

Two years ago, he had stepped off the coach into the noisy heart of London with nothing but crusted boots and the weight of his father's final word. A word he preferred not to repeat, not even in his own mind. The word clung to him. It was a brand he could never outrun, no matter how many shadowed streets he put between himself and the farm.

He had sought refuge in this city, soon realising this was his first and greatest mistake. He had fled the familiar comforts, abandoned the predictable nature of mornings spent with his mother, his father, and his baby brother. Gone were the comforting smells after a spring storm. Gone was the aroma of roasting mutton and garlic that would drift from the kitchen, his mother's speciality.

London offered no such thing as sanctuary. It instead offered a slow, grinding erosion of the soul. The city broke him down, layer by layer, day by miserable day. Its alleyways were narrow and suffocating, choked with coal soot and the eye-watering stench of human waste. A permanent grey film covered everything around him. It coated the walls of his minimal lodging, the clothes of the passers-by, and the back of his own throat. He could taste it, the city, a sour residue that no water could ever hope to wash away. He had prayed too, by God he had prayed for relief, but his prayers remained unanswered. His prayers vanished somewhere between the hacking coughs of citizens, and the mournful wail of ships moving along the Thames. He had no choice. He must continue, there was no other way.

Javier spent his early days pushing through crowds, his mind always returning to that same accounting, the same calculation. What piece of his soul could he barter for the night's shelter? What could he trade for a cut of bread, for the basic privilege of drawing breath? He had tried to find honest work. He had walked until his toenails bled, visiting factory hands, shop assistants, even trying his luck as a butcher's apprentice. Each door had closed in his face. Though, it wasn't long before Javier began to notice a pattern in these rejections. There was a strange consistency in the way people looked at him. Each employer, after declining his services, would linger a moment longer upon his face. They would make some comment about his appearance, a compliment.

He did not yet understand the specific gift that providence had afforded him. He did not understand why men and women alike, would watch him with such hungry eyes, or why they would approach him with whispered propositions as they stumbled out of the taverns at midnight. However, soon, the understanding did come. It was late one evening, his third month in London, when hunger had reduced him to a shadow of himself. He had been scrounging for scraps behind a baker's shop, his fingers numb with wet and cold, when he was approached by a middle-aged foreman. The burly man had emerged from the shadows of the nearby warehouse. His calloused hands had wandered with a greedy confidence, going where they had no business being. Javier had moved to push him away, but then he felt them: cold, heavy coins pressed into his palm, his protestation ceasing willingly.

That was how the ledger began. A ledger of bodies, of transactions, of lust and want. Most of the entries in this new ledger were hurried and graceless. They were arrangements with men whose lives were written in the roughness of their skin; the smiths bore coal stains that were bruised deep into their knuckles, their hands thick as cured leather. The labourers reeked of yeast and soured sweat. The encounters followed a weary, familiar pattern: a muttered proposition in the shadow of a tavern, a figure detaching itself from the mossy embrace of a brick wall. And then the touch. Always artless and impatient. It was a desperate fumbling that spoke of needs they could barely name. Though, in their eyes, Javier always recognised something familiar.

The other trade in the alleys, the other boys, scorned Javier as he collected his coin. For Javier possessed the finest asset, his very beauty. It was the one thing the city could not strip from him, no matter how many stains found their way onto his body. His mother had been dark and his father had been fair, and they had bequeathed him a complexion like that of copper. He was a warm colour against the city's usual offering of sickly, pale boys. He would watch them, scramble and beg, their knees scabbed and their voices thin with whining pleas as they clung to the sleeves of swaying drunks.

Javier laughed as he watched. He laughed and he reveled, and in those moments he felt powerful.

Javier simply had to reveal himself; a slow turn of his head from a darkened doorway or a gaze of feigned disinterest was enough to sever another boy's desperate hold of a patron's forearm. The coins that followed were secondary. For Javier, the real payment was the sting of humiliation on the other boy's face as he was discarded into the dark.

This evening's summons, however, was different. It defied every precedent he had established. It did not arrive as a drunken whisper or a crude invitation. It came in the form of a square of cream parchment, folded with corners so precise they looked like they could part flesh. The woman who approached, moved with a hypnotic, ballet-like fluidity down the alleyway toward him. Her presence was so unusual, that Javier found himself staring, despite his usual wall of caution. Dark curls hung deftly around a face of porcelain, entirely unmarked by the city's grime. Her deep blue coat was immaculate, her shoes, patent black leather, were polished to a brilliant sheen. Now before him, her gaze meeting his, Javier recognised something he hadn't encountered in months of transactions: a complete and total indifference to his physical appeal.

Her eyes held no hunger, no appraisal, no lust. In fact, they held nothing. Abyss. They held only cold calculations, as if she were appraising him, as if she were surveying him. For a moment, he felt her. Inside, somewhere inside, shuffling through his memories. He blinked, hard, his presence now back with her intensity. She made him feel uncomfortably visible.

For a moment, the alley's stench was drowned out by the whisper of her perfume. It was rich and floral, utterly hypnotising. The sensation was intoxicating, but she frightened him. Yet, he could not look away.

The woman offered a brief nod. She extended her hand, the parchment held delicately between velvet-gloved fingers. Javier took it, and without saying a single word, she turned and melted back into the gloom of the city. The encounter had lasted mere moments, yet as he stood there clutching the heavy paper, disbelief mingled with a warming pride.

A woman of obvious breeding had sought him out specifically. Him. He had heard whispers of such invitations, stories of young men being summoned to the private residences of titled gentlemen, but he had always dismissed them as the fallacies of desperate boys. After all, if such arrangements truly existed, surely he would have been the first to receive one? He was, without question, the finest specimen that London's shadow economy had to offer.

As he unfolded the parchment back in the cramp of his room, its contents confirmed its quality. The script was immaculate. It was composed in fine strokes of black ink. The message bore a simple, direct request: THE PRESENCE OF ONE JAVIER, AT THE MANOR OF LORD TISIPHUS, the following evening. The name felt foreign on his tongue, nothing like the crude names of his usual patrons. Javier understood it as a summons from a world he had only ever glimpsed through iron gates and the windows of passing carriages.

The night that followed, Javier prepared himself with the devotion of a priest readying for communion. He had a bar of lavender soap, French-milled and worth more than three days' worth of meals, but tonight demanded that kind of extravagance. He worked the richness of its lather between his palms. Every inch of his skin received his attention. He scrubbed away the city, and with it, the phantom touch of every man who had procured his flesh. The icy water in his basin raised gooseflesh along his arms as he rinsed, then rinsed again. He had purchased a small vial of rosewater from a nervous apothecary, another ruinous expense, and he dabbed it at his pulse points the way he had seen the expensive courtesans do. His fingernails were scraped clean with a small blade until they no longer bore soot. The worn velvet doublet he owned, once a deep ruby, was now faded to the colour of rust. It was the finest garment he owned, and it had to do. He brushed it with obsessive care, picking away every stray thread and speck of lint to the naked eye. He washed his hair twice with the precious soap and combed it until it gleamed like polished charcoal.

When he finally left his room, he carried himself differently. His chin lifted high, his shoulders squared back. The coins remaining in his pocket were few, but his radiance in the mirror had told him the sacrifice was worth it.

***

As Javier climbed the hill toward the residence of Lord Tisiphus, the clang of London's sprawl gradually faded into a quietened whisper. Ancient trees formed a thick canopy overhead as he strode. The manor itself was built of weathered grey stone, its architecture speaking of old money. A well-maintained gravel drive curved toward a set of large, wooden doors.

He stopped before them, immediately drawn to the brass knocker at its centre. The thing was larger than his fist and cast with visceral artistic realism. A woman's face in the brass, her expression frozen in a state of serenity. What he had first taken for elaborate hair revealed itself, upon closer inspection, to be serpents. Their scaled bodies were writhing and intertwining around her features, their eyes open and predatory.

His hand rose toward the knocker, then faltered. Without conscious thought, his thumb found his mouth. His teeth began worrying at the cuticle, a nervous habit he had inherited from his mother. The memory brought with it a sting of pain, jolting him back to the present. He snatched his hand away, disgusted by this betrayal of his composure. He would not show such weakness, especially here.

He grasped the heavy knocker and let it fall. The boom echoed through the manor like a funeral toll. The door was opened by another woman, and Javier felt that same unsettling recognition stir in his gut. Where the first woman had possessed dark, light-swallowing eyes, this one's were as pale as ice. They were a shade of blue so light they seemed almost colourless. Her skin held the same porcelain perfection, as if she had never felt the heat of the sun. Her hair was a severe black curtain that fell straight as a blade past her shoulders. Without a word, she gestured for him to follow and turned into the depths of the manor.

The silence that enveloped them was oppressive as he stepped inside. It pressed against his eardrums until he felt he could no longer bear it. Seeking to break the suffocation, Javier offered a tentative pleasantry to her back as they walked down a seemingly endless hall.

"It is a grand house," he murmured, his voice sounding loud and intrusive in the hushed corridor.

The woman gave no sign that she had even heard him. Her posture remained unchanged. He fell silent, listening only to the tick of unseen clocks and the soft patter of their footsteps on the black-marbled floors. As they moved deeper into the warmth of the manor, Javier was ushered into a library. It was decorated with anatomical charts, rendered in exquisite detail, hanging between towering shelves of leather-bound volumes. Curious instruments made of silver and glass lay perfectly arranged on side tables.

By the fireplace, seated in a chair that matched her companion's rigid posture, was the woman from the alley. She held a book in her lap, her dark eyes lifting to witness Javier's entrance.

Javier was so transfixed by the room's calculated order that he nearly missed the figure rising from the chair opposite her. Lord Tisiphus stood tall, no groan, no click of the bones. He was a man of perhaps fifty years who carried it well. His frame was stocky beneath the fine, dark wool of his tailored coat. His silver-streaked hair was drawn back from a high forehead, centred between broad, strong shoulders. It was his eyes that arrested Javier. They were a startling clear green, like ivy. It immediately reminded him of the cold months in an old life on the farm. They held a penetrating intelligence, a look of calm curiosity that surveyed Javier.

"Master Javier," Lord Tisiphus said with a subtle tilt of his head, his voice incredibly deep. "You are punctual. A rare virtue in these times." He gestured toward the women. "My sisters. They are women of few words, but they are invaluable companions."

Both women offered the briefest of nods, their movements almost synchronised, and without a word, they glided from the room, leaving only the whisper of their fabric, and the echoing click of the door closing behind them.

Lord Tisiphus gestured to the chair opposite his own. "Pray, be seated. There is wine."

Javier moved to the chair, settling into its dense softness. For a long moment, the silence felt laden with curiosity as it hung there. He met the lord's gaze directly, recognising the quiet challenge, refusing to be the first to look away. Tisiphus poured a long stream of deep red wine into a crystal glass. He was smiling, as if the game had begun, as if Javier had passed the first test. The liquid caught the firelight, tiny specs swimming through the stream as it poured. Javier accepted it, his hands intentionally steady.

"Shall we dispense with the silence, Master Javier?" Tisiphus swirled the wine, sitting himself in the seat opposite. "We might speak of the opera, or the popular melodies of the day, but I find such topics tiresome. I prefer stories. The old ones. Tell me, have you read the works of Ovid?"

Javier tasted the wine and felt its warmth spread through his chest. It was richer than anything he had ever known. "I haven't had much time for reading, my lord. Apologies."

Another smile touched Tisiphus's lips. "We find ourselves in a hasty age, so the blame is not yours." He leaned forward slightly, his ivy-green eyes locking onto Javier's. "Tell me of your family."

The wine, the piercing gaze, it was a potent combination that disarmed him completely. He stared into the liquid of his glass for a long moment.

"My father cast me out, my lord. My mother... she took her own life. After my brother died, she couldn't bear the weight of it."

Lord Tisiphus paused, then shook his head with a sympathetic shake. "A lamentable plight, Master Javier. My heart grieves for you." He leaned back into his chair. "Out of curiosity, may I ask which transgression forced your banishment?"

"He did not approve of my nature. For I consorted with a man. He terms it an abomination, my lord."

Tisiphus let out a dry chuckle. "Abomination." He took a slow sip of his wine. "The lament of the modern age. Men cling to their new god, his laws, his commandments. They have forgotten the older ways."

He rose and moved toward the fire, gazing into its flickering light. "The ancients understood justice differently, Javier. They knew that certain crimes demand an answer. Not sins of the flesh, of lust. Nonsense." He turned. "I speak of what is owed when blood is spilled. Do you understand?"

He let the words settle in the quiet room.

"The Greeks had names for the ones who collected such debts. The kindly ones, they called them. A pleasant name for very unpleasant work. Tell me, Javier. Do you believe in a god who forgives? Or do you believe that some acts demand reckoning?"

Javier could only stare, mesmerised. He didn't fully grasp the strange turns of the lord's speech. "I believe in myself, my lord. We are alone in this world. That much I know for certain."

By the time the third glass was drained, the air between them had shifted, with a slow, natural unfolding of intimacy. Tisiphus stood and gestured toward a door Javier had not noticed, hidden between the shadow of two bookshelves.

The chamber beyond was furnished with the same practicality as the library. A large bed, draped in natural linen, dominated the room. Lord Tisiphus's approach was unhurried, almost clinical in its attentiveness. The disrobing felt like an unveiling. His fingers, hot and steady, traced the curve of his collarbone. His hands explored Javier's form as one might study a rare specimen, noting the slenderness of his waist and the smooth, round plane of his buttocks. Each touch carried an intensity that made Javier feel as if he were a statue of beauty being appraised.

First their lips met, then their bodies as they lay. Tisiphus moved with a patience Javier had never known from his usual patrons. Hours passed in that quiet room. When the culmination finally came, it shot through Javier with an unexpected poignancy. He lay afterwards feeling as though something had been taken from him, as well as something given. Though he could not say what.

With the Lord's seed settling within him, and as Javier fought a wine-heavy slumber, Tisiphus pressed a small carved stone box into his hand.

"A trifle," he murmured. "Relish this sweetmeat in the morning, as we partook of ample wine. It shall soothe your mind and your body. Vow to me you will partake of this."

Javier's fingers closed around the box. It was a solid token of a night that already felt like a dream. He gave a small nod before drifting into an uninterrupted, restful sleep.

***

The following morning, back in his room, Javier stared down at the box. The same woman's face from the door gazed up at him from the carved stone, but here, the serenity was nowhere to be found. Her mouth was wrenched open in a silent scream, her eyes pressed shut in agony, tears carved into her cheeks. The serpents still coiled around her, but now they seemed to be consuming her, biting into her temples and her throat. He opened it and consumed the confection inside: a candied peel of some exotic fruit. Its outer layer was hard and sugary, yielding under his bite with a crackle to reveal a juicy interior. The first bite was a rush of honey sweetness, utterly delicious. But as he chewed into the fruit's interior, a violent sourness bloomed, seizing his tongue and the back of his throat. His instinct was to spit it out, but Lord Tisiphus's words echoed in his head, and so, bracing himself, he swallowed.

Javier soon returned to his life, though something had changed. There was a lightness in his step and a strange clarity to the world around him. Smells seemed fine-tuned. The sounds were distinct. He wondered if it was the fruit, or perhaps simply the memory of being wanted by someone like the Lord.

Though, the first wrongness came in the second week. It was a persistent queasiness that clung to his mornings. He dismissed it as bad water or spoiled bread, but it did not pass. By the third week, the nausea had become a constant, nagging companion. And with it came the cravings.

He woke one morning with soil beneath his fingernails. He had no memory of leaving his room, yet his tongue was thick with grit and his teeth were caked with mud. He had been eating the earth. The shame of it made him retch, but even as he spat it out, some primal part of him wanted more.

Then came the evening with his thumb.

He had been sitting on his bed, hunger gnawing at him like a disease, when his hand drifted to his mouth. It was an old habit. His mother's. He began nibbling at the cuticle, feeling the satisfying sting of torn skin. But this time, his teeth did not stop. The pain was secondary. In the moment, there was only a desperate, starving need. His jaw worked, cracking through the nail, through the flesh, and through the wet resistance of the bone. Warmth flooded his mouth. He swallowed.

When the compulsion finally released him, he stared at the ragged stump, blood pooling in his palm. His own thumb sat in his stomach. And somewhere beneath, a memory boiled over: a small hand reaching from a cradle. Tiny fingers grasping at the air. His brother. He forced the image down.

In the fifth week, his belly began to swell.

It was subtle at first. A tightness in his waistband. A tenderness when he pressed his fingers to his stomach. He told himself it was diet to blame, but his clothes grew tighter each and every day.

His patrons noticed. Hands that once roamed freely now hesitated at his midsection, then withdrew in confusion. The work dried up. The other boys in the alleys, who had once watched him with envy, now watched with whispers, laughing behind their hands.

By the sixth week, Javier could no longer pretend. He lay still one morning, watching the light travel across his ceiling, when he felt it. A flutter. It was deep in the strange fullness of his belly. He held his breath. It came again. A tremor, delicate yet unmistakable, like a trapped bird beating its wings.

He knew that feeling. His mother had described it once, her hand pressed to her rounded stomach, her face soft with wonder. "He's moving," she had said. "Your brother is moving. Here, feel."

Javier pressed his own hand to his belly. Beneath his palm, something shifted.

A physician, his last resort, pronounced it a most peculiar tumour of prodigious growth. The prescribed bleeding and purgatives only weakened Javier further, yet the swelling grew. With it came the undeniable sensation of movement. A jostling crawl within, then a sort of deep undulation.

The realisation, when it solidified, was so monstrous it threatened to shatter his mind: he, Javier, a man, was with child. There was no other explanation for such reality, though it felt too unnatural to speak aloud.

There was only one name that tore through his terror: Lord Tisiphus. Clinging to a desperate thread of hope that the lord might undo this curse, Javier resolved to seek him out.

When he finally reached the manor, an icy dread filled him. The windows were shuttered. The polished brass knocker was gone. He found a serviceman's entrance at the rear, its door unlatched.

Inside, the silence was laden with dust. The library, once a sanctuary of intellect, was a cavern of echoes. Books, charts, instruments; all had vanished. Lord Tisiphus and his silent sisters had dissolved as if they were a dream. Javier sank to his knees in the centre of the desolate library. The last of his hope crumbled. He was alone with the impossible, monstrous thing growing within him.

And so it began.

The first spasm of an unimaginable agony ripped through him. His waters broke, a warm, viscous flood soaking his breeches. Labour, a word he knew only from women, had claimed him with unnatural violence. The hours that followed were torment. Each contraction seized his entire being, wringing shrieks from him that were swallowed by the emptiness of the manor, and the surrounding fields of desolate farmland.

He thrashed and flailed amongst the dust. This could not be. Yet the relentless tearing was undeniable. He was being ripped apart from the inside. In his agony, he cried out. The lie he had lived for two years fell away, burned off by the searing pain.

"I beg you!" he screamed. "Yes, I have lied! Yes, I now know that it has been my blight! My casting out was not for the touch of a man! That was my shield... the sin I wore so no

one would see the rot! Forgive me for him! For my brother!"
He choked, and he sobbed, and he convulsed on the floor as
the pain continued its white-hot radiation. "He lies with
worms because of me! He was beautiful, my mother's joy, my
father's pride... a thief in the cradle who stole all their light!
Forgotten... just a shadow in the room where he slept! I can
still see their faces when they looked at him. A love which was
mine, given away! It was not fair! I am sorry! I am sorry for
what I have done! Please!"

He let out another scream, then another, strands of saliva
stringing as he shrieked. "I just wanted them to see me again!
The pillow... it was so soft... I remember the little kicks
beneath... like a bird's wing... then nothing. Silence. I took
their son and I fled. I left them. My mother took herself, and
that was for my own sin! The first monster they bore was their
downfall, I understand this now!"

Sweat beaded, then streamed down his face. "Mother!
Father! I threw your love away! And now this pain... it is my
own making, is it not? My brother, born from my guilt to tear
me apart! Forgive me! Let me go! Please, just make it stop!"

Sounds began to crash through Javier's skull all at once. A
baby's wail, thin and desperate. The groan of a rope pulling
tight, then the creak of something swinging from a beam. A
man screaming, the fury bleeding into ragged, broken sobs.

Then the women's voices crawled out of the dark corners
of his mind. A handful of them, starting low, building. Their
laughter cut through the other sounds, drowning out the
baby's cries and the man's whimpers.

Javier's vision warped. He clawed at his consciousness,
begging for it to stop, but the rage had already taken hold.

His fingers found his navel, now swollen and distended, the skin stretched tight and purple-black. The first puncture came with a wet, sickening pop as he pushed. His fingernails broke through flesh that gave way like an overripe pear.

Blood welled, hot and thick, spilling over his knuckles as he forced his fingers deeper and deeper into the cavity. The torn edges of his skin peeled back with a sound like wet parchment. Muscle fibres snapped between his fingers as he clawed through the layers of tissue, each thrust accompanied by a squelch.

His intestines tangled as he carved a wider opening. The stench of blood mixed with the sour smell of bile and worse things, as his bowel ruptured. Chunks of matter spilled onto the floor. His throat was too raw for screaming now. His eyes were too dry for tears. All that remained was the laughter bubbling up from somewhere deep and broken inside him.

A smile stretched across his face as he scooped handfuls of his own body onto the floor with meaty slaps. Something moved inside the chasm, deep down. Something alive and frantic, thrashing against his torn muscle. His fingers closed around it, feeling tiny limbs kicking, something trying to escape. With a throat-shredding wail, he hauled it free, the creavasse of his body collapsing inward as he pulled, placing the thing onto his bloodied chest. He lay in the slick of his own making, his breath coming in rattled gasps. Then, barely audible, there was a soft cooing. He forced his head down, his muscles screaming in agonising protest.

A baby lay cradled in the ruin of his body. It was perfect. It was unmarked. Tiny fists opened and closed, oblivious to the carnage surrounding it. The baby's head tilted, eyes locking with Javier's. One last tear cleared a path through the blood on his cheek as he stared into those ivy-green pools. His baby brother. His greatest sin. Now gazing up at him.

***

It was not long until dawn spilled across the hills. Sheep bleated in the distance, while Thomas, a stout, elderly farmer, crouched beside his oldest ewe and muttered his morning pleasantries.

"Ready to go, old lady?" he said warmly, patting the creature's head.

As he and his flock made their way over the brow of the hill, the sun's warmth eventually reached the old manor. It was little more than broken stone. Thomas had herded his flock past it for forty years. No one had lived there in living memory. The roof had collapsed before his father was born. And yet the crying came from within. It was the unmistakable wail of a baby.

Thomas stopped dead. Leaving his flock to graze, he began the long trek up the incline, scrambling over fallen masonry and pushing through thickets of bush. The crying led him into what must have once been a grand library. The air was dense with the stench of gore and feces. Thomas's breath caught as his eyes found the scene. A man lay torn open on the timber floor. His face was frozen in a smile. And there, on the deceased man's chest, a baby lay crying. Thomas felt a scream building in his throat. But before it could escape, a woman's voice cut through.

"Be calm, friend."

She emerged from behind him. Her hair was short, dark, but silver-streaked, framing a face of marble-like paleness. She wore a tailored suit of dark, auburn wool. When her eyes met his, Thomas felt something ancient in them. They were a pale, clear green. She moved toward the body with a stride. She knelt and looked down at the dead man's face, tutting.

"A pretty thing, once. It is always a shame."

Thomas could only stare as she lifted the infant, wrapping it in a cloth that seemed to appear from nowhere. She rose, cradling the child, and walked past him without another glance.

He followed her outside, his mind reeling. A black carriage waited on the gravel drive where no carriage should be, for the drive was nothing but weeds and rubble. She opened the door. Inside, two women sat in the shadow: one with dark curls, one with hair straight as a blade. Their pale faces turned toward the infant with warm, maternal smiles. The woman climbed in. The door closed. The carriage rolled forward, its wheels making little to no sound on the broken stones.

Thomas watched until it crested the hill and vanished into the morning light. He stood there for a long time, his flock forgotten, the baby's cry still echoing in his ears.

When he finally looked back at the manor, back toward the dead body of the young man, he could no longer remember why he had climbed the hill at all.

VII

PRECIOUS LITTLE GIRL

precious little girl

Annunciation by Lorenzo Lotto (c. 1534)

DIANA SURFACED FROM SLEEP, every muscle in her body screaming exhaustion. Four hours, maybe. That was all she had managed before Lilly's wailing dragged her back to consciousness. She forced her eyes open, blinking against the grainy morning light. Ryan stood by the window, threading his belt through the loops. From downstairs came Maisy's insistent meow.

"Want me to?" His voice was rough with sleep.

Diana's vision blurred into focus.

"No, it's okay," she murmured, already pushing herself upright. "I've got her."

He nodded, not pressing the matter. He bent down with a groan, they both made sounds like that now, and lifted his work bag from the floor. With a soft kiss pressed to her forehead, he was gone, and once again, she was alone with the crying. Her body resisted every movement; joints clicking and aching in places that had never hurt before, as if childbirth had fundamentally re-configured her skeleton. She caught a glimpse of herself in the mirror as she stood, but left it in her periphery.

By the time she reached the landing, Lilly had quieted, just for a moment, allowing Diana to make her way down to the kitchen.

Cardboard boxes still lined the walls. KITCHEN ESSENTIALS one read in Ryan's block letters. Another corner held BOOKS/STUDY with its contents spilling. Maisy wound between her ankles, her meow rising to an operatic pitch.

"Alright, alright, drama queen," Diana murmured, scooping kibble into the bowl. The cat attacked her breakfast, crunching away as if she had been starved. Diana measured instant coffee into a mug. She took it black as there was no milk left, and listened to the sounds of her cat eating. Then, from upstairs, a soft cry from Lilly's room.

"I'm coming, baby girl," she called, already climbing the stairs.

The nursery door was slightly ajar, just as she had left it. She pushed it open and moved to the cot, softening at the sight within.

Lilly looked up at her with her enormous blue eyes.. Diana lifted her daughter carefully, feeling the warmth settle against her chest. Her weight was perfect. She fit exactly in the crook of Diana's arm, designed for that precise space.

"Good morning, sunshine," Diana sang, bringing her face close to breathe in her distinctive scent. "Did you sleep well?"

A rumbling sound answered her. Lilly always made the most peculiar vibrating noise when content. A happy baby making happy sounds.

Back in the kitchen, Diana practised her delicate choreography of one-handed cooking. She cracked eggs into a bowl, planning on french toast, while Lilly nestled against her shoulder. Maisy had finished her kibble and was now weaving figure-eights around Diana's ankles.

Diana paused, eggs forgotten. "You want to go out, girl?"

After carefully settling Lilly into the bassinet near the doorway, tucking the soft white blanket around her and making sure she was secure, Diana unlatched the front door. Maisy slipped out into the cool Melbourne morning, tail high.

Diana watched her go, then let her gaze shifted to the house next door. Lucia was already in her garden, despite the early hour. She had to be seventy at least, though she moved with surprising strength as she worked her secateurs through a dense rose bush. Her apron, bright yellow lemons on white fabric, was tied around her stout waist. Her back was to Diana, grey hair pinned in a tight bun.

"Morning!" Diana called out, raising a hand.

The snipping stopped. Lucia's head turned, just enough for Diana to see her profile. No wave. No nod. Just a blank stare before she turned back to her roses, secateurs resuming their sharp *snip-snip-snip.*

Diana lowered her hand slowly as two joggers passed, witnessing the brief dismissal. It was nothing, she told herself. Cultural differences. Or maybe the woman was hard of hearing. What a bitch. She retreated inside, where Lilly's soft murmuring sounds pulled her back to their little world.

***

The days collapsed into an endless loop of feeding, changing, snatching fragments of sleep that never felt like enough, cooking, wiping, unpacking, laundry, changing again, feeding again, drinking enough water, making the bed, getting groceries, feeding Maisy, feeding Lilly again, feeding herself.

Evenings brought Ryan home, carrying with his exhaustion, the smell of metal from the garage.

Tonight they ate chicken stir-fry from one of those meal-delivery services that promised "quick and easy" but delivered neither. Ryan picked at his food, eyes fixed on his steamed broccoli.

The only sound that mattered to Diana was the gentle breathing from the bassinet in the corner. She had positioned it where she could see it. Lilly was asleep, her small chest rising and falling.

"Have you met the neighbour?" Diana asked, pushing around the dry chicken across her plate.

Ryan looked up, his focus returning from wherever it had wandered. "Which one?"

She gestured toward Lucia's house with her fork.

"No. Why?"

"Old lady. She hates me.

"What did she say?"

"Nothing."

"Nothing?" He frowned. "Then how do you—"

"This morning, I was outside and I waved. I smiled. You know, being friendly, because I see her out there all the time but haven't said hello yet. Then..." Diana mimicked Lucia's dismissive head turn. "She completely ignored me. Like I didn't exist."

Ryan knew Maisy had probably been digging in the woman's garden; there had been dirt on her paws yesterday. But saying so would lead to an argument they were both too tired for.

"She's probably just private, Di. A bit odd. Don't worry about it." He speared the chicken, his gaze falling back to his plate.

"How was work?" Diana asked.

"Good. Busy."

Diana took a sip of wine, her one glass. "Maybe I should reach out to some old clients. Extra money. And I need... I dunno, I need to do something."

Ryan's head snapped up. "Are you sure that's a good idea? There's no pressure, Di. You should be resting. I don't want you to feel like you need to—"

"I don't know," she interrupted, taking another, larger sip. "Just thinking."

As if summoned by the tension, a wail erupted from the bassinet.

Diana waited. She watched Ryan, watched his hand tighten around his fork, watched him stare at his plate.

He hadn't moved. He hadn't even flinched. The familiar tug of gravity pulled Diana to her feet. She sighed,

"You don't have to—" Ryan tried.

She went to her daughter.

***

The next morning found Diana on the couch, Lilly nursing quietly at her breast. The television droned with some daytime show, bright set pieces that felt aggressively cheerful. The living room was mostly half-unpacked boxes, though Diana had managed to clear a path from door to couch.

Lilly's suckling had fallen quiet, and Diana felt her eyes growing heavy. The warmth against her chest, the gentle pressure, it was hypnotic. Peaceful, even.

Then: shuffling footsteps on the front porch.

Diana's eyes snapped open. She grabbed the remote and thumbed the mute button. The laughter cut off, leaving only silence. She held her breath, listening. The shuffling had stopped.

BANG. The front door shuddered in its frame. Lilly jerked against her chest, letting out a startled cry. Diana quickly adjusted her clothing, gathered her daughter close, and stood.

She pulled open the door.

Lucia stood on the porch, her face twisted with fury. Those dark eyes in the harsh sunlight burned with an intensity that made Diana take an involuntary step back. Before Diana could speak, Lucia hurled something at her feet. A heavy plastic shopping bag landed with a soft thud in the hallway. From inside the bag came a terrified, muffled yowl: Maisy. The cat scrambled out and bolted toward the living room, a grey-striped blur of panic.

"Jesus, what the hell?" Diana gasped, clutching Lilly tighter. Lucia's voice erupted in a torrent of harsh Italian, words Diana could not understand but whose meaning was clear in every jabbing finger, every contorted line of the old woman's face:

"Tieni questo animale lontano dal mio giardino, o ti pentirai di averlo mai lasciato avvicinare a me di nuovo!"

"I don't... I don't understand what you're saying," Diana stammered. "Please, just calm—"

But Lucia was not listening. With a final, venomous glare, she turned and marched back toward her property. Diana slowly closed the door, her whole body trembling now. Lilly was wailing, her small fists clenched against Diana's chest.

"Shhh, baby, it's okay," Diana murmured, but her voice was shaking.

"Maisy?" she called toward the living room. "Mais? Come here, sweet girl."

The cat crept out from under the coffee table, eyes wide and fearful. Diana knelt carefully, still holding Lilly, and extended her free hand. Maisy approached cautiously, then rubbed her head against Diana's fingers. Her purr, when it came, was the quietest Diana had ever heard from her.

"You okay, baby girl?" Diana whispered. The cat just blinked, offering no answers. Diana stood and carried Lilly to the rocking chair, settling in to comfort her. She brought her daughter's face close to her own, feeling the rapid flutter of her heartbeat gradually slow. "It's okay," Diana whispered. "Mama won't let anything hurt you. I promise."

***

Ryan's morning departures continued: a kiss on her forehead, often before she was fully awake, always with that same haunted look in his eyes. Then Lilly's cries from the nursery, demanding Diana's attention. One morning, she lay in bed for a full hour after Ryan left, listening to Lilly escalate from murmurs to full-throated shrieks. It wasn't that she didn't want to go to her daughter. It was that the effort of rising felt insurmountable.

When she finally reached the nursery, Lilly's face was red and tear-streaked.

"I'm sorry, baby," she whispered, lifting her daughter's warm, solid weight. "Mama's here now. I'm so sorry."

Diana was in the kitchen slicing tomatoes for a sandwich. Meditation music trickled from her phone, distant gongs and breathy flutes meant to soothe. Lilly was in her bouncer nearby, making soft cooing sounds. Then, from outside: a shriek. High-pitched and razor-edged with rage. Lucia's voice.

Diana froze, knife suspended over the cutting board. She peered through the kitchen window. She could see the top of Lucia's grey head bobbing among the rose bushes, but not what she was doing. The yelling continued. Harsh Italian, then some violent thuds.

Diana stretched onto her toes, craning her neck, but the foliage blocked her view. Then: *BANG* on her front door. Louder than before. *BANG! BANG!* Lilly began to cry. Diana dropped the knife; it clattered against the cutting board. She hurried to the front door. She stared at the wood that seemed to vibrate with each impact.

BANG. BANG. BANG!

"That's it," Diana muttered, yanking the door open.

Nothing. The porch was empty. The street beyond was quiet. A breeze rustled the leaves. No one there.

***

That evening, Ryan's face was lit by the cold glow of his phone screen when Diana slipped into bed beside him. He was scrolling, thumb moving, his expression empty.

"Finally," Diana breathed, relief flooding through her. Lilly had settled. The house was quiet. She waited for Ryan to look up. He didn't. "You okay?" She nudged him, harder than intended.

He startled, looking away from the screen. "Sorry. What?"

"You seem a million miles away."

"Yeah. Just... exhausted." He scrubbed a hand over his face. "Long day at work."

Diana hesitated, then plunged forward. "I think she's fucking with me."

Ryan's brow furrowed. "Who?"

"Her." Diana jerked her head toward the wall, toward Lucia's house. "The neighbour."

Ryan's sigh was long and slow. He turned to face her, reaching for her hand. "She's just a strange old woman on a quiet street, Di. That's all." His voice was soft. "Just relax. I can almost guarantee she isn't fucking with you." He squeezed her hand gently, making little circles on her thumb with his. "It's going to be sunny tomorrow. Why don't you get out for a bit? Fresh air. It'll do you good."

He was looking right at her, his focus absolute. The suggestion was delivered with such careful sincerity, as if sunshine was the obvious cure for everything wrong. The words felt like a dismissal. Like he wasn't hearing her. Diana felt heat flush through her chest, but she swallowed it down.

"Maybe," she said quietly, turning away. "Yeah. Maybe I will."

***

The park was busier than Diana expected. Children shrieked with laughter as they chased cockatoos across the grass. Parents called out warnings and encouragement. She sat on a bench, one hand on the pram, rocking it gently back and forth. With her free hand, she attempted to eat a cheese and Vegemite sandwich. Lilly was asleep inside the pram, her tiny face serene beneath the canopy. She scanned the park, observing the other mothers. They looked so capable, so energised. How did they do it? What secret did they know that Diana had somehow missed?

She took a bite of her sandwich, and that was when she saw her. Far across the grass, near a dense cluster of eucalyptus trees at the park's edge, a woman perched on a low branch. Not sitting. Perched. Like an oversized bird. Her limbs were drawn in, her dark dress bunched around her, and her head was tilted at an unnatural angle. It was her eyes that caught Diana's attention. Even from this distance, they were fixed and unblinking.

Lucia.

The figure moved. Not the careful, joint-popping descent of an elderly woman. She dropped to the ground on all fours, knees and palms hitting the dirt with distant thuds.

For one horrible instant, her body settled low to the ground, spine curved, head thrust forward.

Then she began to run. She stayed low, scuttling across the grass with impossible speed. Her hands were splayed wide, her fingers clawed. She dug into the turf, propelling herself forward. Her legs, tucked beneath her, pumped like machinery. Her dress snagged and tore on the ground. Her head was thrust forward, chin nearly scraping the grass. Diana could see teeth. Bared. White and sharp. It was a relentless, horrifying advance. Directly toward her. Toward the pram. Toward Lilly.

Diana tried to move. Tried to stand, to grab the pram, to run. But her body had turned to stone. Her muscles locked. No sound would come.

The thing that looked like Lucia was close now. Close enough that Diana could hear the rasp of her breathing, could see the lemon-patterned apron dragging in the dirt. Then a man pushing a bicycle crossed between them, his young daughter chattering excitedly as she walked alongside.

When they passed, Diana's gaze snapped back to where Lucia had been.

Nothing.

Just dappled sunlight through the leaves. Just the ordinary sounds of children playing on a Tuesday afternoon.

Diana's hands shook so violently she could barely unlock the front door. She pushed the pram inside and immediately went to check on Lilly in the nursery. Her daughter was still sleeping, miraculously calm. Diana watched. *She's alive, she's safe, she's here*, before returning downstairs. Maisy wound around her legs, but Diana barely noticed. Her mind was replaying what she had seen on a loop. *It knows where I am. It can find me.*

She spent the rest of the afternoon setting up the security cameras she had finally unpacked from their box. When Ryan came home, he found her in the living room, laptop open, eyes fixed on the screen. The display was divided into four sections: front porch, hallway, kitchen, nursery.

"Di?" His voice was careful.

"I set up the cameras," she said, not looking away from the screens.

"Why?"

"For her. To keep an eye on things. To keep Lilly safe."

Ryan looked from the screen to his wife's rigid posture. He opened his mouth to argue, to reason, to say something, but closed it again.

He should call someone. He knew he should call someone.

But the thought dissolved as quickly as it formed, replaced by that familiar hope that tomorrow she would be better. That this would pass.

"Okay," he said quietly. "Okay, Di."

He went to shower, and the water did nothing to wash away the cold.

***

Every time Diana closed her eyes, she saw it: the four-limbed scuttle, the bared teeth, the lemon-patterned apron dragging through dirt.

When Ryan left for work, Diana was already on the couch, cold tea beside her, laptop open. The hours crawled by. Sun tracing shadowy paths across the carpet. Her heart leapt with every movement on the screens: a plastic bag skittering down the street, Maisy slinking along the fence line, the postman across the road, joggers passing by the house, cars slowing and parking, kids playing with a soccer ball, birds on the porch.

From upstairs, Lilly's whimpers grew steadily in pitch and intensity. Diana's eyes never left the screens. The whimpers became cries. The cries became shrieks.

And then Diana saw it. A flicker on the kitchen camera. A swift, dark movement near the window.

Lucia. Crawling. Slithering through the narrow opening Diana could have sworn was closed.

Diana watched as the dark shape flowed across the kitchen floor like liquid shadow, then disappeared from view.

Heading for the hallway.

Heading for the nursery.

Heading for Lilly.

The scream upstairs intensified: raw, terrified, piercing. But she didn't run toward the nursery. She ran to the kitchen. Her hand closed around the cool, heavy handle of the chef's knife from the block on the counter. She raced upstairs, taking the steps two at a time, knife gripped. The nursery door was open. The crying had stopped. Silence.

Diana stepped inside. Her gaze swept the room: the cot, the walls, the...

There. In the corner where the two walls met the ceiling. A dark shape. It was Lucia, but wrong. Her body was impossibly high in the top corner of the room. The black fabric of her dress had stopped being cloth. It stretched and pulled like dark limbs, thinning into appendages that held her there. The fabric splayed into long fingers pressed flat against one wall, anchoring the impossible shape.

And from the center of this dark thing, two eyes. Staring down at Diana. Wide and unblinking. Lucia's eyes. Diana raised the knife. Her body became a rigid shield in front of the cot where her daughter lay. She did not move. She did not breathe.

The thing's mouth opened.

And opened.

And opened.

A silent, tearing void that stretched beyond all reason.

From that void came a sound: a wet, rattling growl. The sound of a rabid dog, feral and hungry.

Its head began to shake. Violent, thrashing, left to right so fast the shape blurred. The growl erupted into explosive barks.

Diana's throat tore open. A single piercing shriek ripped through the quiet suburban afternoon. A sound of pure, animal terror, before cutting into sudden silence.

***

The flashing blue and red lights painted the front of the house in alternating colours that evening. Someone had heard the scream and called the police. Ryan's car screeched to a stop at the curb. He ran up the path to find Diana on the top step of the porch, wrapped in a blanket. She was rocking back and forth, her small bundle held tight to her chest.

"Shhh, shhh, it's okay," she was murmuring, her voice hoarse and broken. "No more crying. Shhh. Mama's here. Mama's got you."

"Diana?" Ryan's voice cracked. "Jesus, what happened?"

Before she could answer, a uniformed policewoman approached. "Are you Ryan?"

He nodded, tears welling in his eyes.

"If you wouldn't mind coming inside for a moment."

He followed her into the house, his heart threatening to burst. The living room was exactly as it always was: boxes in corners, blankets strewn about. He felt suddenly hyper-aware of how half-moved-in they were. The laptop sat open on the coffee table, its screen paused on camera footage.

The officer pressed the trackpad. The footage was from the upstairs camera, even though it read 'nursery', it was just the spare room, stark and empty. Never got to use that room. In the center of the frame stood Diana, a large kitchen knife held in both hands, blade pointed at the ceiling.

Her face was slick hot with tears, her eyes twisted in terror, locked on an empty corner where two walls met the ceiling. The timestamp showed she had been standing there for two hours and forty-seven minutes. A sob escaped Ryan. He buried his face in his hands, but he couldn't unsee it: the knife, the empty room, the nothing she was fighting.

"I'm sorry to ask. But... When did you first notice changes in your wife's behaviour?"

But Ryan couldn't answer. Because he was seeing it now. Or maybe admitting what he had been seeing all along.

The park. It always came back to the park. A year ago. The elderly woman walking her dog near the eucalyptus trees. The dog, a large mastiff, breaking free from its leash. The frantic, terrible moments of the attack. The screaming. The blood. Ryan hadn't been there. But he had lived Diana's fractured account of it a thousand times since.

This: the knife, the phantom in the corner. This was her mind's attempt to rewind time. To stand guard in a battle that had already been lost. The unbearable weight of not being able to protect their daughter had curdled into this. And he had let himself believe she was getting better. The quiet days, the lack of tears, the way she went through the motions. He had mistaken numbness for healing. He had wanted so badly to believe they could move forward that he had ignored every sign.

The officer was still speaking, but Ryan couldn't hear her. Couldn't hear anything except the echo of Diana's scream and the memory of his own cowardice. When he finally emerged from the house, the cool did nothing to calm the fire in him. Three officers filed past him down the path. Car doors slammed. Engines started. The blue and red lights swept across the neighbouring houses one final time before the street returned to its ordinary suburban darkness.

Ryan's gaze was drawn to Lucia's house. She was standing beside her rose bush, wrapped in a dressing gown. Their eyes met across the distance. She had called them, he realised. The kindly old woman who had never been anything but pleasant in the handful of times they had actually spoken. Who had probably watched Diana's deterioration with growing concern. Who had finally called for help when Diana wouldn't.

She held his gaze for a long moment, and then a small, sad smile touched her lips. Then she turned and retreated into her home, closing the door quietly. Ryan's attention returned to the only thing that mattered. He sat beside Diana. She was still rocking, still murmuring soft reassurances to the bundle in her arms.

"She's finally settled," Diana whispered, her voice fragile. She looked up at him, her eyes clouded but calm. "She's safe now. I kept her safe."

Ryan looked down at the bundle wrapped in the blanket, Lilly's blanket, the one they had chosen together before she was born. He could see the gentle rise and fall of breath. He reached out and laid his hand on the breathing figure. From under the blanket, that familiar rumble. Maisy's chainsaw purr, loud and insistent and alive.

Ryan felt the last of his strength crumble into an aching clarity. All the questions, the frustrations, the weary dismissals; they all evaporated. He looked at Diana. At the hollows beneath her eyes. The way her thumb stroked the fur in small circles. At the woman he had married and loved so fiercely, holding onto the only warmth she could find in a world that had taken everything else.

He didn't offer empty words. He didn't try to correct her or pull her back to a reality she couldn't face yet. He simply slid his hand over hers, their fingers intertwining around the soft warmth of the cat.

Their purring, precious little girl.

And together, in the darkness, they rocked.

VIII

NUTRIPASTE SUPREME

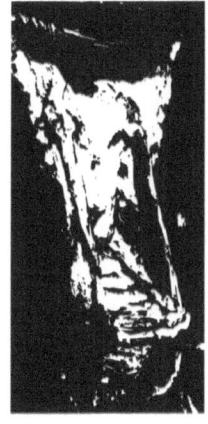

nutripaste supreme

The Slaughtered Ox by Rembrandt (1655)

NUTRIPASTE SUPREME: EDIBLE CHICKEN PRODUCT. The lone cursor blinked against the sterile white of a barely-touched document. Sarah's fingers hovered over the keyboard like a pianist who'd forgotten the next note. She was reluctant to give this "product" the dignity of elevated prose.

She read the title again, breaking the syllables down into unpalatable, bite-sized pieces: NU-TRI-PASTE SU-PREME

Another assignment, another test of her dwindling endurance. The product was a culinary abomination, and her task was to find anything worth saying about it, for a readership that wouldn't know the difference between the real thing and this grey slurry anyway. Sarah pictured them, her readers: their palates dulled by years of engineered proteins and chemical enhancers.

There was a time when the name Sarah McKinnon had actually meant something. Chefs would emerge from their kitchens to greet her personally. Restaurateurs held tables just for her. Winemakers sent their finest bottles, hoping for a mention that could make or break an entire vintage. She'd spent years chronicling genuine flavours: the way a proper chilli built heat with a slow, symphonic burn, or how fish caught that morning still carried the ocean's spray in its buttery flesh. She'd loved it once. The writing, the tasting.

That enthusiasm now felt as distant as the invitations themselves. Those tables weren't held anymore. The bottles stopped arriving. And Sarah couldn't remember the last time she'd written about food with anything resembling joy.

Because now, eight years into the MIOD-C mandates, she was paid to find new ways to describe the 'textural nuances' of whatever the city's protein synthesisers shit out each season. She recalled a dollop of grey matter that was meant to be beef, squeaking against her teeth as she chewed. She had described it as possessing 'a surprisingly robust mouthfeel'. She let out a deep...

deep...

deep

sigh.

"Monday blues, Sarah?" A frustratingly familiar voice chirped from behind her. Sarah forced a corporate smile before turning. Jane from admin stood there beaming, her round frame drowning in a lumpy, hand-knitted cancer of a cardigan.

"Just working on an article," she replied, maintaining the mask of her office smile. "Trying to find a way to describe this NutriPaste thing. Another one. Can't say I've had the pleasure of trying it yet. Have you?" She wouldn't have been surprised, in fact, she was practically bracing for Jane to announce it was her new favourite protein.

Jane leaned over Sarah's shoulder to squint at the screen, bringing her signature bouquet with her: cat urine and sweaty inner-thighs. How does a person not know they smell like that? Sarah wondered, peering up at the pale, soft expanse of Jane's double chin.

"Oh! Hubby said the NutriPaste Ultra was lovely!" By some miracle, she leaned back. "I wouldn't trust his judgement, though. That man eats the Sardine variant, the one that looks like those little plastic fishing lures, and he bloody loves it. Can't stand that stuff". Jane's breathy chuckle made Sarah's temples tense up. How this woman had managed to find a husband was one of the city's great mysteries. "They keep coming up with the most bizarre names. 'Ultra', 'Supreme'... what's next?"

Sarah then reluctantly imagined Jane's husband: a specimen who likely considered tomato sauce a valid serving of vegetables. She offered a hum.

Jane's voice dropped into a cloying whisper. "Tonight's the night, isn't it? The date?"

Sarah's stomach gave a lurch. It was partly Jane's lack of boundaries, but mostly it was the looming reality of the date itself. She had mentally filed the event under her other tedious obligations, nestled somewhere between her private health insurance renewal and a cervical screening. But Breanne, her editor, had somehow twisted Sarah's disdain for such an archaic concept as a 'blind date', into reluctant acceptance.

"He sounds gorgeous, Sarah. His name is Daniel. Tell me with all honesty: have you ever met a Daniel who wasn't hot? Exactly." Breanne had chirped early last week. "And he's worked with Mark Noye! You know Mark, his taste is impeccable." Before Sarah could muster a reasonable excuse, Breanne had organised the meeting.

Mark Noye. It was a name that carried the kind of weight Sarah's used to. His taste was his most sacred currency, and he wouldn't devalue it by endorsing someone common. An architect Sarah had interviewed once, after designing a new Japanese fusion place in town, back when meat was actually meat. He was cold, rude and told Sarah that her questions regarding his process were 'juvenile, at best'.

"It's just dinner, Jane," Sarah said, shrugging and swivelling back toward the blank document.

"At Harvest, though? That's not 'just dinner'! How did he even manage to get a table? Hubby and I tried for our anniversary, we had to book a year in advance when the place first opened. Absolute madness." Jane's eyes widened.

"Crazy, yeah," Sarah mumbled, typing a string of nonsense across her screen in a desperate attempt to look busy.

Still, Jane had a point. That was the other lure, alongside Noye's endorsement: Harvest. It was more than a restaurant; it was an institution, one that operated far outside Sarah's current reality of faux meats and bland flavours. It was an establishment so elusive that a reservation required the kind of social leverage Sarah no longer possessed.

"I want a full report on Monday! Especially if he's as steamy as Bre reckons." Jane's conspiratorial wink made Sarah want to punch her square in the nose. The last person Sarah was going to divulge the intimate details of her life to was Jane from admin. Sarah managed a nod, watching as the woman shuffled back to her desk, mercifully waddling from view.

Finally alone, she turned back to the blinking cursor. Taste, Sarah reflected, separated people more effectively than wealth or education. It determined who belonged where, and who deserved what.

The mere thought of spending an evening with someone who might describe wine as 'yummy,' or someone who saw nothing wrong with Jane's cardigan, made her physically ill. She needed to reclaim what the name 'Sarah McKinnon' once stood for. Her signature had been polluted, affixed to articles praising industrial abominations and tissue cultures until her byline became synonymous with schlock.

There was still time to fix it, she convinced herself, time to scrub away the stain of every NUTRIPASTE review and restore her reputation. She wanted people to hear 'Sarah McKinnon' and think only of one thing: taste. Pure, unimpeachable taste.

***

Sarah stood before her bedroom mirror, smoothing the silk of her black dress, a brutally expensive piece that murmured of quiet elegance. She'd deliberated for an hour. Her red blouse felt too eager, and her blue slip felt too severe and desperate.

She spritzed herself with Louis Vuitton Pure Oud, a gift from an old client she'd been rationing since the onset of her moral decline, and made her way out of the apartment.

It was a chilly night, her arms wrapped tightly against her frame to ward off the bite of the evening air. Thankfully, the ride-share arrived quickly, and she was immediately assaulted by the sting of cigarettes as she climbed inside. The grey-stubbled driver twisted to greet her, unleashing a wave of damp, stale breath directly into her personal space.

"Sarah?" he gargled, eventually returning his gaze to the road as he clocked the destination on his phone. "Oh, Harvest! Damn, very nice." His thick fingers left the wheel as he spoke. "I've read things about their food. Change your life and all that." He coughed, mouth wide open. Sarah instinctively held her breath. "You know, I used to be in the food business myself. Real food."

He began to drive, weaving through the traffic with the erratic confidence of a Balinese cab driver. "Twenty years in cattle farming. Good land, happy animals. Bloody good life it was. Then, y'know, MIOD-C happened." He shook his head, his hands leaving the wheel to punctuate every word with a frantic gesture. Sarah had always loathed people who spoke with their hands.

"They gave it the most science-fiction name possible. That's because it *is* bloody fiction. All bullshit, pardon my language." He glanced at her in the mirror, searching for a nod that wasn't coming. "They said overseas.... what? That the feed was all contaminated? That there were tumours in the livestock? Pssht! Every news channel, every morning, showing you sick animals while you tried to eat your cereal. Scared everyone senseless. Bloody worked too."

He shook his head again, finally returning both hands to the wheel as he took a corner too fast. "Funny thing is, I never saw a single sick cow on my property. But guess when I did? When the inspectors came. After they came, I mean."

Sarah fixed her gaze on the passing city lights, silently begging for the traffic to yield. His voice dropped to a hushed stage-whisper. "Then, suddenly, the labs have all the answers. Grown proteins, cloned this, synthetic that. Perfectly safe, they tell you. No disease risk, they tell you. Then... Bam! They hijack the entire supply chain." He leaned toward the mirror again, his eyes wide and unblinking. "You can't tell me that wasn't the plan all along. You want to control the population? You make them scared of their own food."

Sarah wished he'd focus on the road. His conspiracy was as stale as the car's recirculated air. She was paying for transport, not a front-row seat to these bitter ramblings.

The car slowed, finally. "Right then, here you go. Appreciate five stars."

"Thanks." Her hand sought the door handle, but a sudden, chilling doubt arrested her movements. She knew almost nothing about Daniel Wright. What if he was merely a more expensive version of this driver? A man with cut-price theories, who gesticulated wildly and smelled of fresh garbage. The possibility made her stomach clench.

Oh God, what was she doing?

"You alright, darl?" the driver asked, his voice thick with unearned concern.

She focused on the restaurant. It was unremarkable from the outside, just a narrow, unmarked door of brushed steel wedged between a nondescript art gallery and a bespoke tailor. There was no neon, no desperate advertisements; only a small, discreetly lit plaque bearing a stylised sprig of rosemary. An establishment like Harvest was precision-engineered to filter out men like her driver.

"All good, thanks," she murmured, already mentally logging a two-star review for the odour alone, as she stepped out into the night. A fresh ripple of nerves fluttered, not for the date itself, but for the building.

In just a year, Harvest had become an institution. The whispers were always vague but intense, hinting at obsessive chefs and a religious devotion to sourcing the highest-quality ingredients. She had too much pride to grovel for a table like some amateur blogger. Instead, she had simply waited on the outside.

But tonight, she was finally on the right side of the threshold. The door glided open before she had even reached it. A tall, slender man with raven-black hair and a flawlessly tailored suit nodded with practiced grace.

"Welcome to Harvest. We're thrilled to have you." He bowed his head slightly. "My name is Gabe. I will be looking after you this evening. Please, come this way."

He led her through a series of softly lit, interconnected spaces divided by panels of smoked green glass and dark, polished wood. The air was warm and rich, a complex perfume of woodfire, exotic spices, and the deep, primal scent of roasting meat. Low conversations drifted from unseen tables. Subdued lighting casted orange glows that seemed to fade in and out slowly while she approached the booth. It occupied the room's far end, a secluded alcove of dark green velvet.

"Your table, Ms McKinnon. Mr Wright should be with you shortly." Gabe gestured with a subtle sweep, a crisp linen cloth draped over his forearm. Sarah offered a faint nod and settled into the softness of the booth. From her vantage point, her gaze was immediately drawn to the kitchen. It was visible through a pane of reinforced glass: a theatre of chefs in pristine whites, moving with a controlled fluidity. There was no shouting, no clatter of steel, only a hypnotising ballet of absolute focus. In the minutes she sat watching, not a single one of them looked up.

A shadow detached itself from the periphery of her vision, and suddenly, he was there. Daniel Wright. The name felt suddenly inadequate. He was taller than she'd anticipated, with broad shoulders that spoke of a disciplined physicality, all tailored into a deep hunter-green wool suit. His orange hair was expertly cut, framing crystal blue eyes, full pink lips and a smooth, pale complexion.

"Sarah." Her name left his lips with a polished baritone. His eyes drifted from her face, tracing the lines of the black silk dress before returning to her gaze. "That dress is beautiful. You look elegant." The compliment was a precision strike, aimed not at her body but at her discerning eye. It had disarmed her so potently, she had not realised she was standing, as if she were a supplicant waiting for her blessing.

"You're too kind," she replied, her voice consciously steady, slowly sitting again. She nodded toward the glass. "I was admiring the discipline."

A slow smile spread as he settled into the booth opposite her. "It's pretty impressive isn't it? That level of focus is almost alien these days."

"I haven't seen that sort of thing in a very long time," Sarah said, finding herself leaning instinctively toward him. "When a team of chefs barely speaks like that, you know they're doing it right. Like artists. Artists don't need to talk." Sarah let out a small, self-conscious chuckle, covering her mouth with her hand. "Sorry."

Daniel regarded her for a long moment, his eyes alight with an obvious, shared attraction. "A food writer who actually laments the loss of craft. You are a rare breed. I've kept up-to-date with food literature, and it's exhausting. Nothing exciting, nothing new, or even real anymore. Harvest though." He leaned back, eyebrows raising.

"I can't lie," she admitted, "these days, I write about what I'm paid to write about, unfortunately. And it's not all golden, let me tell you."

Before she could elaborate, Gabe appeared at the edge of the table. His arrival was so silent he seemed to simply manifest from the shadows. He offered no menus.

"Mr Wright, welcome, it is a pleasure to see you again, and I do apologise that I did not greet you personally when you arrived," Gabe said softly. "The chef recommends beginning with the Consommé. And tonight's sourcing for the main course is a particularly fine cut and preparation."

Daniel nodded, his eyes never leaving Sarah's. "And to drink?" He gestured with a nod toward her. "Their cellars are extensive. Any preferences?"

"Surprise me," Sarah said.

Daniel's smile widened, revealing teeth that were white, complete, and perfectly aligned. He murmured a vintage and a vineyard she surprisingly didn't recognise, and then Gabe vanished back into the gloom.

Once they were alone again, Daniel leaned forward. "So, Sarah McKinnon, food writer. I have to confess, I've read some of your recent work." He smiled, and Sarah's own expression faltered. "Tell me: what does a woman who writes about mediocrity for a living, actually care about?"

The question was so clinical, so devoid of first-date preamble, that Sarah couldn't help but laugh. "God. We're skipping the small talk entirely, then?"

"Small talk is for people with nothing to say," he replied smoothly. "And I have a feeling you aren't one of them." He had bypassed the tired script, the questions about her apartment, her career, her upbringing, and aimed for something more fundamental.

"Well. My greatest fear is losing my sense of quality. Of taste. The ability to distinguish what is genuine from what is passable. It's as simple as that. I want to be reminded why I love food, why I ever bothered to write about it in the first place."

His eyes gleamed. "Then you've come to the right place."

The first course arrived with a silent flourish. The consommé was served in a bone-white porcelain bowl. A pool of flawless, yellowish liquid, completely translucent. The aroma was a direct assault on her current career, not the acrid, chemical sting of replicated broth, this was palpable. There were gamey notes layered over a sweetness she couldn't quite place.

Sarah lifted the bowl, her hands warming against the fine porcelain. The first sip of the broth was a pure revelation. A clean heat warmed her palate, not with oiliness, but with a mouth-filling subtlety. It carried the richness of bone marrow, of time and patience. If this, Sarah thought, was any indication of the skill Harvest offered, she was on the precipice of a night she would never forget.

She set the bowl down, her hand trembling ever so slightly. "Extraordinary," she whispered.

"Isn't it? The ingredients are remarkable, as is the preparation. Most people have forgotten what real food tastes like," Daniel remarked. Sarah was midway through savouring another mouthful, a sudden flash of self-consciousness striking her.

"Their palates are dulled by synthetics, by lab-engineered flavour profiles," he continued. "They crave sugar and salt because they can no longer discern subtlety." He dabbed a glisten from the corner of his mouth with his linen napkin.

Sarah nodded, Jane's vacant praise for the NUTRIPASTE echoing in her mind.

"They've been conditioned to settle for the 'faux' in everything," Sarah added. "Faux meats, faux fats, faux flavours. I remember when I was a child, God, I hope this doesn't make me sound ancient, but substitutes were exclusively for vegans and vegetarians. Processed soy products, meat alternatives for people with actual dietary restrictions. Looking back, it was a gateway drug. Now, everyone's palate has been hijacked. It's devastating."

"I remember it well. It's a shame we can't all afford luxuries like this. Perhaps we're just lucky, or..." Daniel's gaze held hers. "Perhaps it's a matter of taste. You can't buy taste, after all."

The next course arrived: a small, artfully composed mound at the plate's centre. What appeared to be finely diced mushrooms had been precision-cut into near-perfect cubes, their earthy surfaces glistening with oil, scattered with charred fragments. Delicate microgreens crowned the preparation alongside glass-like wafers. A dark, glossy reduction pooled around the base like ink.

Sarah took a careful forkful. The texture was extraordinary, the tender mushroom yielded under her teeth with a familiar umami richness before transforming into something flesh-like. Daniel watched her reaction with obvious satisfaction.

As the plates were whisked away with seamless efficiency, the young waiter appeared once more, his expression a mask of neutral professionalism. "Mr Wright, Ms McKinnon," he murmured, his syllables crisp and perfectly articulated. "The chef will be plating your main course shortly. Now, as is custom for first-time guests," he offered a professional smile, "he extends an invitation. Would you care to view the kitchen suite before your final course?"

Anticipation spiked through Sarah. She glanced at Daniel, seeking a signal, as if asking for permission. "Up to the lady, of course," he said, his smile lingering. The waiter turned his gaze back to Sarah, waiting.

"We'd be honoured," she said, nerves threading through her. The waiter bowed slightly. "If you will follow me."

He led them through a discreet door toward the rear of the restaurant and then into a short, sterile corridor lined with gleaming stainless steel. He paused before a heavy, seamless door and pressed his thumb to a glowing biometric panel. With a short hiss, the door slid open.

"The Kitchen Suite," the waiter announced, his arm extending in formal welcome. Sarah stepped across the threshold, Daniel close behind. This was no kitchen, it was a fusion of a surgical theatre and a high-spec abattoir.

Gleaming steel tables stood in immaculate rows. Upon them, instruments lay; knives of every gauge, heavy cleavers, and bone saws with fine, carnivorous teeth. Then, she saw them.

Suspended from overhead rails by hooks driven through their achilles tendons, a dozen carcasses hung in a row. They were skinless and stripped down to muscle. They varied in size: some were small, almost delicate, others were larger, meatier.

There was no question. The forms being so artfully dismantled were human.

Sarah felt no surge of nausea, no primal scream of denial. Instead, after the initial, jagged lurch of recognition, her standards began an appraisal.

Sarah's gaze shifted to the chefs. They worked with the same focused grace she'd witnessed through the glass. She watched as one younger chef made an incision along a pale flank. It was a masterful act of deconstruction.

Limbs were disarticulated at the joint with something akin to tender care. Torsos were opened by a master's hand, the skin yielding to reveal the detailed architecture beneath.

Gabe gestured toward a smaller, more delicate form with the quiet pride of a curator. "This specimen was sourced from a specialist rural commune," he murmured. "Organically reared, of course. The diet is strictly regulated to ensure tenderness and a subtle flavour profile. As I'm sure you're aware, Mr Wright, we manage every facet of the provenance ourselves."

In the biting stillness of the suite, the weight of Daniel's gaze became evident. She turned her head slowly, finally wrenching her eyes away from the rhythmic work of the chefs to face him. Daniel hadn't been watching the display. He had been watching her.

He had been waiting, gauging the exact moment the shock would dissolve, waiting to see what would remain in its wake. As her eyes met his, he didn't find frantic, tearful denial. He found the discerning clarity of an equal.

Gabe moved toward a larger carcass, its flesh a deeper crimson than the others. "And for your main course, a selection from this specimen. A mature donor, butter-fed throughout its final cycle. The flesh has been dry-aged for twenty-eight days to break down the enzymes. Note the superior intramuscular fat along the primary cut." He ran a gloved finger lightly over the flank, almost as if he were caressing fine silk. "Exceptional."

Daniel stepped closer to Sarah, his hand finding the small of her back. "Impressive, isn't it? The absolute commitment to quality. No compromises."

Sarah found her voice. "Where do they come from?"

The waiter turned slightly, his professional mask flickering for a fraction of a second. "Forgive me, Ms McKinnon. It isn't our custom to discuss donor specifics or individual provenance. All you need to know is that our sourcing ethics are as meticulous as our butchery."

He gestured toward a nearby section where refrigerated glass cases displayed various cuts, each labelled in elegant script: Ribs, Smoked, Tenderloin, Prime Cheeks, Slow-Braised. It looked like an exclusive boutique butcher's counter, the kind found in the luxury food halls of London or Paris.

An older, female chef worked with precision at a central steel station, deftly shaving paper-thin slivers from a cured leg suspended in a traditional ham-clamping rack. She proffered a translucent ribbon of meat on the tip of her carving knife to Gabe, who then extended it toward Sarah.

"A preview of our charcuterie," the waiter murmured. "Air-dried for eighteen months. Sourced from a donor noted for their exceptionally active lifestyle." Sarah stared at the glistening sliver of reddish-pink flesh skewered on the steel. It was beautiful, a deep garnet hue that paled to white at the edges. She realised, in that very moment, that the chefs ceased. They stared, all of them, at least fifteen. Waiting.

Her entire career had been a relentless pursuit of flavour, of a lost authenticity. She had spent years lamenting the bland, the synthetic, and the mass-produced nonsense of the modern world. Here, held out on a blade's edge, was the ultimate organic product. It was the antithesis of NUTRIPASTE. It was real. And it was waiting for her.

She took the sliver of cured flesh, it was cool and feathery, weightless against her fingertips. Daniel watched with unblinking intensity.

Sarah raised the meat to her lips, the aroma drifting up, delicate, saline, and haunted by a sweetness. She hesitated for a heartbeat, before letting it settle onto her tongue.

It was a symphony of salt and concentrated umami, followed by a faint, metallic copper note. It dissolved almost instantly, a phantom of pure flavour. It was, without qualification, the most exquisite thing she had ever tasted. A soft, involuntary hum of surrender escaped her. The chefs continued working, several of them with a subtle smile playing on their lips.

Gabe offered a shallow nod of professional vindication. "I'm so glad you enjoyed it," he said softly.

Returning to the amber sanctuary of the booth felt like stepping back into a dream. Sarah's perspective had undergone a fundamental shift. The plush velvet and the golden, diffused light were no longer just decor, they were a necessary and beautiful veil draped over a truth she now carried within her.

Gabe returned. He placed a large, silver cloche in the middle of the table. Its handle was adorned with a green gemstone of some kind.

"The chef's signature preparation," the waiter announced. "Slow-roasted at a precise temperature. Served with a reduction derived from its own rendered fats and marrow, accompanied by glazed heritage carrots and a parsnip fondant." With a flourish of theatrical finesse, he lifted the cloche.

A plume of steam escaped, carrying an aroma so profound, so concentrated, and so impossibly rich, that Sarah felt dizzy. She stared down at the plate.

The presentation was, as with every preceding course, impeccable. Nestled against a velvet-smooth parsnip fondant were the heritage carrots, glistening with a lacquer of glossy, dark reduction.

It wasn't the heritage vegetables that held her gaze, they were merely the supporting cast. To the side of the artfully arranged garden, occupying the silent, significant portion of the plate, was the centrepiece.

Steamed. Unmistakable. A human head.

It was presented facing her, its features set in a state of meditative repose, eyes closed. The skin had become pale and opalescent, turning slightly translucent under the heat of the steamer. It had been cleaved down the centre, a neat, bloodless line revealing the pearly white of the cranium beneath the veil of flesh. A gentle plume of steam rose from the crown, carrying a scent that was sweet, robust, and undeniably meaty. It was garnished with a single rosemary sprig, tucked with artistry behind the curvature of one ear.

Heat surged into the back of Sarah's throat.

Daniel picked up his knife and fork. "An honour to be served this cut," he murmured. "The true test of a chef's skill is utilising the entire donor. Waste is the ultimate vulgarity, don't you think? It shows a lack of respect for the provenance."

He made a precise incision into the cheek of his portion. The flesh parted with buttery ease, revealing a texture that was pale, dense, and perfectly uniform. "The cheek is particularly succulent," Daniel noted, lifting a forkful, placing it on a small serving plate and nudging it toward Sarah.

Sarah looked down toward the single mound of cheek on her plate. He caught her eye and offered a small, encouraging smile. "Don't be shy, Sarah."

Her hand trembled, only slightly, as she reached for her silver-heavy cutlery. She stared at the steamed head, the rosemary sprig tucked behind the ear. But as she looked, the trembling changed its nature. It wasn't the frantic vibration of fear or nerves. It was suspense.

She was salivating. Her body, primed by the aroma and taste of the charcuterie, had already accepted the product.

Slowly, Sarah picked up her fork. She didn't see a face anymore, she saw a map of flavours, a challenge of texture. The moment she chewed, the moment she savoured the warm, rich juices spilling from the cheek, it was there. Unmistakable.

The flavour was refined, but it carried that persistent, underlying bitterness. The structural acidity of a man who had spent his life perfecting an unforgiving, elitist palate. This was no ordinary donor. This was Mark Noye.

A surge of satisfaction swelled in her chest, more intoxicating than the wine. She remembered the way he had looked at her during their singular interview, the way he'd let a silence hang just a second too long before explaining, with excruciating patience, how her questions could have been 'better framed'. He had treated her like a child, a novice in a world of high-concept architecture.

Now, that same architectural precision was laid bare on her plate. The man who had looked down on her was now providing the most exquisite, authentic dining experience of her life. He was no longer a critic or a rival, he was sustenance. He was flavour. She swallowed.

She looked up at Daniel, her eyes bright with welling tears. She didn't need to say the name aloud, it was written in the lingering, bitter finish. Daniel leaned back, his smile widening to reveal those perfectly-aligned teeth.

"He always did have a rather... robust opinion of himself," he murmured, his voice laced with shared amusement. "Did you know him?"

Sarah didn't respond, she just continued. Soon realising she cleaned her plate with professional focus. She had been offered the remaining head, navigating the bone until only the pale skull remained as a silent witness to her appetite.

When Gabe returned to offer coffee, the transition was seamless. Both Daniel and Sarah declined with a shake of the head. The atmosphere of the room seemed to finally exhale. There was no need for the bitterness of coffee to wash away the experience, she wanted the taste of Noye to linger.

Outside, the Melbourne air was an antiseptic shock after the warmth of the restaurant. Daniel called for her car, and as they waited under the glow of the streetlights, he studied her face with a quiet intensity.

"You are quite extraordinary, Sarah McKinnon," he said softly. For a moment, the space between them tensed with the possibility of a kiss, a standard conclusion to a standard date. But when the car pulled to the kerb, Daniel simply opened the door for her, and made no move to follow.

She rode home in silence, the complex finish of Mark Noye still lingering on the back of her tongue.

***

Sarah woke the next morning in her own bed, but the return to her life was a jarring descent. The morning light now felt artificial, streaming through the window to reveal a life she no longer recognised. The familiar drone of city traffic felt like static.

Her phone buzzed on the bedside table. A text from Breanne, a frantic string of capital letters and exclamation marks: HOW WAS IT?? WAS HE AMAZING?? CALL ME!

Sarah stared at the screen. The message felt like an insult, a vulgar intrusion from a woman who existed entirely on the surface.

With a hand that was perfectly steady, Sarah deleted the text. Then, she deleted Breanne's contact entirely. Her resignation email, sent an hour later, was entirely devoid of sentiment or excuse.

Words seemed meaningless. She was no longer interested in descriptions. She had tasted the real article, and the faux world had nothing left to offer.

Daniel hadn't asked for her number. Of course he hadn't. To have done so would have been a descent into the very small talk he despised. The night wasn't a prelude to a relationship, it was the entire transaction. It was a singular, perfect event designed to permanently ruin her for anything else.

The thought was parasitic. She kept seeing Mark Noye's face. She found herself imagining the texture of his lips, the way the delicate cartilage of his nose yielded with a satisfying pop between her teeth, like Imperial Beluga caviar. Not even the luxury of such a product came close anymore, even when it was the real thing.

For seven days, she lived in the afterglow of Harvest. Every other sensation was muffled, like a radio tuned to static. Each morning she checked her phone, but Daniel's silence was absolute. A damning verdict.

On the eighth day, as her obsession curdled into resignation, she found the unlisted booking number for Harvest. She left a message. Not for a table, but for him. She waited through silence, and then, the phone vibrated in her hand.

"Sarah. What a surprise."

"Daniel," she said, her voice low. She hadn't eaten in days. "I've been thinking about our date."

"It was a memorable evening," he replied. "Truly. But I think it's best if we leave it there."

"I'm not calling you for a second date." Sarah paused, the silence on the line stretching as she contemplated the triviality of his assumption. To think she was interested in something as pedestrian as a second date was almost insulting. "I'm calling to make a donation."

A silence, sudden and buzzing with static, fell over the line.

"I want to be on the menu," Sarah continued, her voice gaining an edge. "I am the source Harvest would admire. I have spent my life cultivating a palate that the world has tried to dull. I am, and will be, the epitome of good taste."

The silence finally broke with a soft, slow chuckle of genuine admiration. "Well, Sarah McKinnon," Daniel said, "that is an extraordinary offer. I will get you in touch with Gabe immediately."

***

Gabe and Sarah's meeting was not conducted over wine, but across the polished mahogany of a lawyer's desk. Gabe was different now, immaculately dressed as always, but his demeanour had shifted from hospitality to logistics. His eyes assessed her with the gaze of a liquidator.

The lawyer, a thin, desiccated man with silver hair and thick-lensed glasses, spoke in a drone of legalese. He used phrases like "voluntary asset transfer," and "post-mortem property rights." The documents she signed, dozens of them, were masterworks of euphemism. They didn't speak of death or butchery, they detailed "final vesting," "total asset liquidation," and "biological provenance." Her signature appeared again and again.

"The preparation diet is quite specific," Gabe explained, "It has been designed by the executive chef personally. No deviations will be permitted. Not a single calorie is left to chance. I am sure you understand the necessity."

"And the timeline?" Sarah asked. She felt an electricity beneath her skin, an eagerness for the process to begin.

"Eight weeks," Gabe replied, his pen scratching across the final documents. "Depending, of course, on how precisely you adhere to the programme." He paused, looking up from the mahogany desk. "There are psychological support services available, should the reality of the vesting period become... taxing."

Sarah laughed. The idea that she would need 'support' to achieve her own masterpiece was absurd. "I don't think I will."

Gabe smiled then, the first genuine, human expression she'd seen from him all day. "No. I don't think you will either." It was the coldest, most clinical transaction of her life, and as she looked at the ink drying on her own death warrant, she realised she had never felt more vital.

The apartment Harvest provided was a statement of intent. The design was instantly recognisable as the work of Mark Noye, or at the very least, a disciple who worshipped at his altar of his trademark perfection.

The minimalism was absolute. Every line was severe. Every surface was so pristinely clean, it felt medical-grade. It was a space engineered for purification, designed to strip away every extraneous detail of Sarah's previous life, until only the essential remained. Floor-to-ceiling windows framed a Melbourne that now seemed distant and muted. The pale timber floors were bare and polished to a mirror-like sheen. The few pieces of furniture looked less like they were built and more like they were rendered; perfect, geometric forms that offered no concession to human comfort.

It was in this pristine cage, three days after her call, that her preparation began. The routine was strenuous, yet for Sarah, it was meditative. It was the first time in her life she didn't have to judge, she only had to be. Each morning began with blood tests administered by a silent, white-clad technician who arrived at precisely seven-thirty.

Her meals arrived in heavy stainless-steel containers at exact intervals: breakfast at eight, lunch at one, dinner at seven. These were not 'dishes' in any traditional sense. They were calibrated preparations of nutrients and essential minerals, designed to systematically flush her system and imbue her flesh with a superior flavour.

The food was a triumph of engineering, yet utterly devastating in its blandness, the gastronomic equivalent of white noise. Proteins that possessed the texture of silk but the flavour of air, vegetables that looked like vibrant jewels but tasted of nothing, grains that dissolved on her tongue like distilled water. It was the most expensive, highly-designed fuel she had ever consumed, crafted by a genius to ensure that not a single external flavour would contaminate the profile of her own flesh.

On Friday, and then every Friday from then on, the silence was broken by the arrival of the massage therapist, a woman with hands like iron and a detached efficiency. She worked Sarah's muscles with a punishing depth, kneading her body for hours on end. "For tenderness," the woman would murmur, when Sarah's breath hitched. The goal was the systematic breakdown of lactic acid and the prevention of any stress in the tissue.

Isolation was the final ingredient. No phone, no internet, no digital static. Just a curated library of philosophy and gastronomy. She spent her hours reading Brillat-Savarin and Heidegger, marbling her mind with high-concept thought. If Harvest was to serve "The McKinnon," the essence had to be as refined as the anatomy.

After a week, she noticed the absence of reflections. There were no mirrors, no polished chrome, not even a dark window-pane that hadn't been treated with a matte, anti-reflective coating. She asked the technician about it, the silent woman who moved through the space like a ghost. For the first time, the woman paused, her gloved hand hovering over a blood vial. She looked at the blank wall, then at Sarah, and delivered the only words she would utter during the entire stay.

"Better for the process."

Sarah understood their reasoning immediately. They wanted to prevent her from becoming self-conscious. They didn't want her to recoil from the physical reality of her refinement: the way her skin was thinning to a waxy sheen, or how her hair now came away in clumps in the shower.

It wasn't the decay that angered her, that was a beautiful, necessary part of her biological unmaking. Her rage was reserved for the fact that she was being robbed of the view.

She was becoming a masterpiece of provenance, and they had forbidden the artist from witnessing the creation.

Daniel visited only once, in the fifth week.

By that time, the erasure was nearly complete. Every trace of the old Sarah; the hair on her head, the arch of her brows, the fringe of her lashes, had vanished. What was left, eyes stark and enormous within the hollows of her skull. Her skin was a luminescent veil, so translucent that the delicate, blue-purple web of her veins were clearly visible. She could sit for hours, mesmerised, watching the pulse of her blood travelling through the architecture of her arms and legs.

Daniel's eyes gleamed when he entered. He approached her, his voice dropping. "You are absolutely perfect. I knew it the moment we met. I knew you would understand what the others could never."

The praise landed with a prickle of irritation. He still didn't get it. Despite his money and his status at Harvest, he was still watching the performance from the safety of the audience. He was a philistine, merely salivating from the sideline while she sat at the chef's table.

He crossed the expanse between them and knelt by her chair like a widowed woman bereaving a grave. When he covered her hand with his, the touch was hot, offensively so. "To witness this... your commitment," he whispered, his thumb tracing the blue, delicate lines of the veins on the back of her now see-through hand. "To be this close to the source..."

Sarah looked down at his thumb, observing the clumsy friction of his skin against hers. This was what he wanted? This desperate, physical reaching? His desires were as mundane and pedestrian as anyone's. He was just another Jane.

She withdrew her hand from under his, meeting his confused, wanting gaze with a pitying calm. "Daniel, please..." she said. Her voice was thin, but carried the absolute authority of a teacher correcting a child who had failed a lesson in their ABCs. "You look pathetic right now. Go away."

It was the last time she ever saw him.

On her final evening, Sarah received her last visitor. The head chef arrived personally, carrying a wine bottle. He was a small, intense man with dark eyes that spoke of a deep European lineage, a man whose ancestors had likely served kings and tyrants alike. He wore civilian clothes, a simple black sweater and dark trousers, but he moved with the same control she had recognised through the glass of the kitchen suite.

"Ms McKinnon," he said, setting the bottle on the geometric coffee table. "I wanted to thank you personally. What you are doing... it is truly an honour, a privilege, my dear. You are providing the context for my finest work."

Sarah gestured for him to sit, her movement fluid despite her frailty. "If you don't mind my asking, I am quite curious about something. The preparation diet. I hope I do not offend you, as it's merely a question borne from professional curiosity. But, as someone who has dedicated her life to the pursuit of flavour... the meals themselves. They tasted of nothing." She looked at him, her enormous, stark eyes searching his face. "They were technically perfect, yet they were a sensory void. Why?"

His eyes lit up with a sudden professional enthusiasm. "Oh, indeed. You see, taste is merely chemical signals translated by the tongue. A blunt instrument. Flavour, however, is memory, smell, neural processing." He smiled, sitting beside her on the rectangular couch. "Those meals were designed to erase your palate's preconceptions entirely."

He studied her translucent face. "I've never worked with such a willing collaborator, one who approaches this regime with such professional curiosity. Most of our donors are... significantly less enthusiastic about it." He giggled.

"Most of your donors aren't food writers," Sarah replied, her voice a dry rasp.

"Precisely, you appreciate the craft, the time, the absolute effort required for a masterpiece."

His gaze shifted to the bottle of wine, a luxurious vintage. His joints groaned as he stood, but before he reached for the cork, he opened a small, weathered leather case. From its lining, he withdrew a large, curved needle.

"I'm afraid," he said, his voice a tone of apologetic professionalism, "that the final preparation requires the oral cavity be sealed. We cannot risk any bacterial contamination or enzymatic interference in these final hours. Purity is paramount. I am sure you understand."

He threaded the needle with practiced efficiency, the twine a coarse, organic twist. "It is a crucial step in maintaining the integrity of the sourcing. I tend to undertake this task personally. I find it... intimate. Imperative."

Sarah nodded. "Of course. Where do you want me?"

"If you could just lie back," he instructed gently. "This will only take a moment."

Sarah lay back on the couch, her eyes fixed on the unforgiving white of the ceiling. The needle was surprisingly gentle, sliding through the skin of her lips with an impressive efficiency. She felt minimal discomfort, her body was already so distant and refined, that pain felt like a secondary, irrelevant sensation.

She watched the chef's face as he worked. He made tiny, even stitches, each one a perfect, symmetrical mark of his dedication. Sarah was deeply impressed.

"There," he whispered, knotting the final stitch, snipping the excess with tiny scissors. "Perfect." He removed his surgical gloves and gave a gentle clap as he admired his work.

He then gestured to the wine bottle, his hands steady. "Now, I believe it is time for us to enjoy this together. What do you say?"

He uncorked the vintage, the scent of dark fruit immediately blooming in the space. While the wine began to breathe, he reached into his kit once more, this time producing the clear, coiled tubing of a medical IV.

Sarah watched, mesmerised, as he drew the wine into a glass syringe with a slow, steady pull. The liquid was a deep ruby. He added it to the IV bag, and she watched the liquid swirl through the clear saline solution, a beautiful, blooming cloud.

"This may feel unusual," he warned, his voice softer now. He inserted the needle into the crook of her arm, the blue-purple vein a perfect, clear target, and adjusted the drip rate with a dial. "But even with the oral cavity sealed, you should be able to appreciate the profile."

The effect was profound. It was an epiphany. The wine's complexity bloomed from the inside out, radiating through her entire system. She felt the rich, earthy notes spreading through her veins like a warm, liquid secret.

The tannins, the bruised dark fruit, and the subtle, charcoal-smoke.

"Extraordinary, isn't it?" he murmured. "It will enhance the final flavour profile beautifully. The final touch. I can barely contain my joy."

Sarah closed her eyes, surrendering to the internal tide of the vintage. She felt the wine course through her.

The Chef closed his notebook with a soft, final snap of leather. His dark eyes were alight with a professional peace. "Tomorrow will be... exceptional," he whispered, as if speaking to a sleeping child.

As he gathered his case to leave, he paused at the threshold of the room. He turned back, his expression softened. "I want you to know, this will be the finest work of my career. You are not just providing ingredients, Ms McKinnon. You are providing inspiration. You are the first donor who has ever truly seen the plate from the other side."

After the door clicked shut, Sarah lay perfectly still. She felt the wine's finish lingering in her system, a long, complex aftertaste. It would be the last thing she would ever taste, she realised.

It brought no fear, only a sense of completion. She had spent her life in a frantic pursuit of truth, and now, she was saturated with it.

Behind her expertly sealed lips, Sarah McKinnon smiled. It was a perfect vintage to close a life dedicated to the pursuit of perfect taste.

***

Several weeks later, the air in Harvest's exclusive dining room sat with its usual understated elegance, charged with unseen excitement from the kitchen and wait staff.

At table seven, the restaurant's most coveted vantage point, Marcus Brighton, the burly, red-faced heir to a mining empire, sat in anticipation. Beside him, his bird-like wife Elena watched, her surgically-enhanced features remained frozen in a mask of poised expectation.

The chef himself emerged from the kitchen. It was a rare appearance that sent a ripple of hushed awe through the room. He moved slowly, personally carrying a heavy silver cloche. He approached table seven with the same reverence as a priest.

"Mr and Mrs Brighton," he announced. "Today, we offer a truly unique sourcing, a donation from a woman who dedicated her entire existence to the study and mastery of flavour." He paused, letting the gravity of the moment settle over the table. "We present: The McKinnon." He gripped the green-gemmed handle, and lifted the cloche.

"Oh, Marcus," Elena whispered, her voice barely a breath. "Look at her."

The chef's eyes gleamed with an artistic fever. "I believe this will be remembered as my masterpiece. I have not yet tasted it myself. I bestow that honour upon you, Mr Brighton."

Marcus Brighton, a man who had audited the world's finest kitchens from Tokyo to Johannesburg, lifted his heavy silver cutlery. He carved a precise portion of the cheek, noting with professional approval the way the meat yielded, it possessed a tender, liquid resistance. He placed the morsel in his mouth and began to chew.

At first, his expression was one of closed-eyed concentration, the look of a man navigating a complex map of flavour. But as his jaw worked, up, down, up, down, something shifted. He was being led somewhere dark. His brows drew together. He slowed his pace, his tongue searching for the refined profile the chef had promised, only to find something far more aggressive.

Elena watched, her anticipation curdling into anxiety as her husband's face contorted. "Darling?"

Marcus set down his fork with a clink against the porcelain. "Chef," he said, his voice dropping. "The texture is appalling. Grainy. And the aftertaste..." He shuddered, a visceral reaction of the body. "Metallic. Bitter. Like sucking on a rusted coin. This is shameful."

The colour drained from the chef's face. "I... that's impossible," he whispered, his voice cracking. "The preparation was perfect. Every detail... the programme was absolute."

"Whatever preparation you used," Marcus interrupted, "has produced something inedible. This is not cuisine. This is an insult."

The chef stammered an apology and retreated, his composure completely shattered. He rushed back through the doors into the kitchen. The line cooks and sous-chefs stood frozen, their eyes wide, staring like mice caught stealing cheese.

With shaking hands, the chef raised a small, squared portion of the meat on a silver tasting fork. He placed it in his mouth, his eyes closing.

The flavour was everything Brighton had described. It was bitter. An aggressive, alkaloid stinging that bypassed the palate and triggered a gag reflex. Beneath the metallic top-notes, there was a distinct, underlying chemical hit. It was the taste of industrial preservatives, of synthetic binders, of something akin to poison.

His professional composure, a mask he had worn since his apprenticeship, dissolved into abject horror. It was a catastrophe. The eight-week purification had done nothing but strip away the water and the fat, leaving behind a concentrated, toxic essence.

He spat the morsel into a white linen napkin.

Within an hour, the usual ballet of the kitchen had devolved into a forensic cleanup. The sous chefs worked in a heavy silence, their movements stripped of their usual artistry. Every trace of The McKinnon was purged from the prep areas and walk-in coolers.

Nothing was salvageable. The product was denied the dignity of being repurposed as a lesser cut, ground for a staff meal, or even donated to the city's food rescue programmes. To do so would be to spread a contagion.

In the pristine, stainless-steel kitchen, the industrial grinder roared to life. This machine, typically the instrument of Harvest's signature artisan sausages, was now tasked with a different form of deconstruction. Piece by piece, the remains were fed into the cold, churning steel. Eight weeks of meticulous preparation, the massages, the wine infusions, the architectural isolation, were reduced in seconds to an unsellable, bitter sludge.

The resulting mince, a grey-brown slurry weeping a sickly, iridescent liquid, was quickly sealed in doubled heavy-duty bags. Even the kitchen staff, hardened veterans, worked in grim silence behind filtered masks and nitrile gloves.

By midnight, the bags were wheeled out to the cobblestone alley behind Harvest, joining the restaurant's waste collection. The bins, sleek and stainless-steel, stood in the narrow lane, shielded from the Melbourne drizzle.

By dawn, one of the bags had been torn open by a persistent scavenger, and a reddish-brown puddle had begun to pool on the stones, mixing with the morning's light rain. A stray tabby cat, thin and street-smart, approached the pool with cautious interest. It sniffed the air, its whiskers twitching. Then it took a single, tentative lick.

Immediately, the animal recoiled. It hissed, shaking its head violently as if trying to rid its tongue of a burn. Its fur stood on end, and it backed away into the shadows, leaving the puddle untouched.

"Maisy! Oh, Maisy, there you are!"

Jane hurried down the alley, her fluffy pink slippers squelching through the puddles. She was wrapped in a faded orange dressing gown. She scooped the tabby into her arms, pressing the cat against her chest. "Oh, you naughty girl! I was so worried! We've been looking for hours!"

Barry, Jane's husband, emerged from the other end of the alley, shivering in boxer shorts, thongs, and a stained football club jumper. He was breathing heavily. "Bloody finally, you little shit," he called out, then stopped dead. His face twisted into a mask of disgust. "Jesus fucking christ. What died over here?"

Jane, still cooing at Maisy, finally caught an involuntary whiff. The colour drained from her face. "Oh, wow," she breathed, covering her nose with the sleeve of her gown. "That smell... Barry, it's exactly like that awful paste, remember?"

"Which one? There's been heaps of dodgy ones," Barry gagged, pulling his jumper over his nose.

Jane bounced the cat absently, her eyes fixed on the grey-brown puddle by the bin. "The 'chicken-flavoured' one. The one that made everyone sick, that huge lawsuit! Shit, what was it called again?"

IX

FOMO

FOMO

The Cottage by Vincent van Gogh (1885)

BZZZZT. Another bloody goddamned motherfucking text message. She didn't need to see the screen, didn't need to unlock it to know it was Tessa again, reminding Ruby of how her Tuesday night was utter bullshit. It was probably another snap of someone doing a shoey, captioned with something like, MADDEST NIGHT, WISH U WERE HERE RU!!!!

Ruby decided to ignore it. She was not in the mood. Year 12 end-of-exams parties. The one they've all been talking about since Year 7, guessing who'd suck whose dick, planning the pre-drinks and kick-ons.

Alas, Ruby was here. Not there.

Here, on the durry-scented, brown corduroy lounge that had been old when her mum was still around. Her dad's bullshit rules were still ringing in her ears: *If I'm out, you're in. No arguments.* Tonight, he was out. The RSL, probably, sinking pints with his workmates. So Ruby was in.

On the small television, Jodie Foster was a child trying to be an adult in The Little Girl Who Lives Down the Lane. It was one of Dad's. "A classic thriller, Rubes," he'd said, tapping the sun-worn DVD case. "Right up your alley. Bit of mystery, bit of spook." The only mystery was why the wallpaper in the movie was so disgustingly orange. The only spook was the realisation that this was the pinnacle of her Tuesday night. The little girl in the movie, Rynn, had secrets. Ruby thought that was hilarious.

BZZT. BZZT. BZZT.

A rapid-fire notification. Probably a group chat now, everyone chiming in. Ruby imagined the photos; dance floors, someone crying in the toilets.

"Ugh, shut up." She slapped the phone screen-down on the lumpy cushion beside her, the vibrations now muffled against the fabric.

She tried to pull her attention back to the movie. Rynn was talking to the creepy landlord, her composure way too adult. "Some tea, Mr Jacobs?" Rynn said.

Ruby absently scratched at a patch of dry skin on her elbow. The restlessness was building, the FOMO an electrical current inside her. It wasn't just about missing a party; it was about missing life itself. It was so unfair.

Her gaze roamed around aimlessly: the fridge in the kitchen, with a bunch of bills and photos and pamphlets stuck on it; her school jumper, a blob of navy blue, slung over the back of the only other chair in the lounge room. She couldn't believe her dad had bought that chair from the op shop, this single-seater ugly-ass thing with stripes all over it. But that didn't matter. Nothing mattered tonight. She was completely alone and everyone was having fun and it was bullshit. Maybe she should study for her English trial. Or sort her uni application. Or literally anything else.

Her pointless thoughts were interrupted. A faint scraping sound from outside. It was coming from the window in her bedroom, just down the short hall. *Possum, probably, maybe.*

But then: *CRASH.*

The sound was immediate. It genuinely startled her. *Not a possum, nope, shit.* That was the shatter of glass, followed by a heavy impact inside her bedroom. Ruby was on her feet before her brain had fully processed it, the remote thudding to the floor. The lounge cushion with her phone on it slid after it. Her heart kicked into a panic. She stabbed the mute button on the telly, plunging Jodie Foster's pale, serious face into silence.

The sudden quiet in the house was immense. She listened carefully, standing as still as possible.

Another sound: a muffled curse word, a stumbling footstep from the short, dark hallway that connected her bedroom, the bathroom, and the lounge. Someone was in the house.

Shit. This was real. Here. Now. *Shit. Shit. Shit.*

Her first instinct wasn't to scream. It was a sweep of the room. She needed a weapon. The heavy glass ashtray Dad never used? No, too small. Kitchen. Knife? Her mind raced, sifting through a lifetime of Dad's more colourful 'be prepared' anecdotes, usually involving situations far more outlandish than a random breaking into the house. A shadow peeled itself away from the black of the hallway entrance, eventually morphing into a person.

Tall, but with the emaciated build of a drug enthusiast. Hoodie pulled so low it shadowed his eyes. Black trackies, stained and torn. He moved with a hesitant energy, like a glitchy robot. He took a step into the lounge, and the TV screen caught his face. Maybe twenty-five, but he looked like he'd lived twice that. His eyes were the worst part when Ruby saw them: wide and skittish, like a cornered animal.

This is bad. This is really, really bad.

He saw her then. Froze for a second, a flicker of surprise in his burnt-out, bloodshot eyes.

"Fuck, yeah... fuck, uh, you good?" he rasped all at once. His voice was a gravelly whisper.

Ruby stayed rooted in front of the lounge, standing like an idiot. The initial shockwave of adrenaline was fading.

"Not really," she managed, her voice steadier than she expected. "Pretty sure you just fucking broke my bedroom window?"

His head swivelled, taking in the meagre contents of the room. His movements were quick and nervous. "Money? What've you got?"

Ruby let out a humourless breath. "There's no fucking cash here." She gestured vaguely at the general air of poverty evident in the lounge room.

His eyes, like two dark holes, snapped back to her. "Don't be a fucking smart-ass."

Ruby took a tentative step back, her calves touching the lounge now. "I'm being honest. No cash."

He advanced onto the carpet, his trainers scuffing on the worn lino that extended from the adjoined kitchen. She could smell him, a rancid cocktail of unwashed body and cigarettes. "Everyone's got something," he insisted, his voice rising a notch. "Jewellery? Phones? What've you got?"

Ruby's gaze flicked to the ancient PlayStation 2 under the telly, then back to him. "Got a PS2. Help yourself. Haven't touched it for years."

He barely glanced at it. His attention was elsewhere, his eyes darting around, finally settling on her again. Then they slid past her, towards the kitchen. "In there. Move." He motioned his head towards it, sniffled hard.

"What for?" she asked.

"Just fucking do it!" he snarled.

Ruby jumped. He took a more decisive step that brought him too close for comfort.

The front door was to her left, but he was blocking the most direct path. Her bedroom was a definite no-go. The kitchen was a tiny, dead-end space. Not ideal. But arguing seemed like a fast track to getting hurt. So, with her legs feeling a little shaky, she moved towards the kitchen area, acutely aware of him following. The lino in the kitchen was cracked and freezing under her bare feet.

"Money," he said again, his voice right behind her now. She could almost feel his hot breath on her neck. "I know there's something. Don't lie, cunt. These fuckin' houses all have cash from deals and shit. Where?"

She turned and leaned against the laminate counter. "I'm telling you, hand to heart, we have no fucking money. We don't touch drugs. Fuck's sake." She groaned, which she shouldn't have done.

"On your knees," he breathed, his voice now flat and dangerous.

"What?"

"You heard me. On the fucking floor. Now."

This was different. This wasn't just about him wanting stuff anymore. A new dread began to seep into her, far different from the initial shock. It was a primal alarm bell.

Run. Should she run? Should she just bolt to the door? But Dad had locked it. He'd locked it before he left and she would have to fumble around before getting out and raising the alarm.

This guy is a real pain.

"I don't think so," she said.

His hand, grimy and trembling, dipped into the cavernous pocket of his hoodie. It emerged with a deliberate motion. It held a cheap steak knife. Cheap, yes, but definitely sharp. The blade was scuffed and stained.

"I said," he repeated, his voice a menacing growl, "on your fucking knees."

Right. So this was happening.

The dominant fear, the one that made her insides queasy, still wasn't about the knife itself, or even dying. It was something else. Something connected to the inconvenience, the potential for an unholy fucking mess, the breaking of far older, far more important rules than her dad's curfew. It was the fear of what this idiot was about to unleash.

With a small, almost inaudible sigh, she lowered herself onto the lino. The cold seeped through her jeans instantly, and a sharp crumb from her dad's breakfast toast dug painfully into her kneecap.

He shuffled closer, the knife held loosely by his thigh. He was too close. He crouched down, bringing his face uncomfortably level with hers. His eyes, pupils dilated to black little discs, roamed her face.

"That's better," he whispered, a faint, unpleasant smile appearing at the corner of his chapped lips. He leaned in further. God, his breath. For one hideous moment, she thought he was going to kiss her. His free hand came up, not to strike, but to rest with a gentle pressure on her shoulder. His face was inches away.

And in that tiny, claustrophobic space, with the reek of him filling her senses and the weight of his hand on her shoulder, Ruby moved.

In a blink, her head raised, then snapped forward. Teeth, no longer blunt and even, but suddenly elongated and needle-sharp, found their mark. They punched through the worn fabric of his hoodie, through the skin and muscle of his neck, sinking deep into the pulsing warmth of his artery. A choked gurgle was torn from his throat, a sound of bewildered terror. Ruby barely registered it. Her own senses were filled with an explosive symphony. At the first taste, her eyes shifted to complete darkness, the whites, the blacks, all consumed by an abyss.

The dull, nagging ache of the FOMO, the gnawing boredom: all of it was consumed, obliterated by a far more urgent hunger. The taste never dulled. A rich, coppery, vital heat that sang through her mouth, electrifying every nerve ending in her body. He began to thrash, a wild, panicked bucking against her, his hands flailing, clawing at her head, at her face, whatever he could grab. The knife, his symbol of power moments before, was plunged into her shoulder, but she did not relent. He twisted it, pulled it out, plunged it in again. Nothing. She shifted her weight, pushing him to the ground, the knife clattering to the lino, forgotten and useless.

Ruby held fast, her jaw locked, drawing him in, drinking deep. His terrified heartbeat pulsed against her teeth, only servicing the bliss that consumed her. The struggles weakened, became sporadic twitches, then just a faint tremor. Finally, with a long exhalation, he went limp, a dead weight under her.

She released him from her mouth. A ragged breath, something like an inhale after downing a milkshake, tore through her own lungs. Her lips were slick and warm. The front of her t-shirt was completely soaked. She could feel the heat of him, rapidly cooling now.

She sat for a moment, her face poised towards the ceiling as she savoured the last vestiges of his life. The tap in the kitchen drip, drip, dripped. Then, from the lounge room floor where her phone lay abandoned:

BZZZZT. BZZZZT.

Ruby slowly turned, her neck stiff. Tessa. Had to be. She could imagine the selfie: Tessa, tongue poking out, a crowd of laughing faces in the background. *OMG RU! YOU ARE MISSING OUT! WISH U WERE HERE! XOXOXO!* Ruby turned her head again, and looked down at the man sprawled. His eyes were wide, but completely vacant, staring up at the ceiling with a look of permanent surprise. His hoodie was a dark, glistening mess around his throat.

The distinct scrape of a key in the front door lock. Her head snapped to her side.

Dad. Shit.

He fumbled his way in. She could smell the cigarettes and beer already.

"Ruby? Still awake?" He blinked as he entered, his eyes struggling to adjust to the dimness. "Jeez, it's like a bloody tomb in here. Thought I told you, early night, school tomorr —"

He stopped dead.

His unfocused gaze drifted from Ruby, kneeling on the kitchen floor, to the crumpled form beside her, to the dark, spreading stain on the lino. His expression shifted.

He let out a sigh. Not a gasp of shock, or a shout of alarm. A sigh. A long-suffering, put-upon sigh. The kind of sigh he reserved for when she used up all the hot water. His gaze flicked to her face, and she felt the last of the black receding from her eyes.

"Ruby, for fuck's sake," he said. "We just ate. Last Thursday." He prodded the dead man's ankle with the toe of his worn work boot. "I've told you, we can't just go eating whenever the fuck we want. There are rules, and planning, mate. Discretion, remember that word?" He gestured vaguely at the body. "This is not fucking discreet."

Ruby slowly got to her feet, her knees protesting. She wiped her mouth with the back of her hand, smearing the sticky warmth across it. "He broke in, Dad," she explained. "Smashed the window in my room. He had a knife and everything!"

Her dad grunted, unimpressed. "Yeah, yeah. Self-defence is one thing, an all-you-can-eat buffet is another." He rubbed at his face. "The point is, this is unscheduled. And it's... fuck, well, it's messy, isn't it? And bloody hell, you're gonna have to tell Nan we're not gonna eat next week. She got it all prepared and everything. Fuckin' hell, Rube." He looked from the corpse, to the spreading pool, then to her bloodstained t-shirt. "You started him." Ruby's stomach gave an unhappy gurgle. Not with hunger; it was the heavy, sluggish feeling of overindulgence. "So you're going to have to finish him," Dad announced, already turning away, making a beeline for his bed. "And properly this time. No bits in the green bin." He moved towards his bedroom door.

"Dad! Seriously?" Ruby protested. "I've got double maths tomorrow!"

Her dad paused at the door, one hand on the frame. He didn't turn around. "Ruby. Now." He pushed through and the door closed behind him with a soft click.

"And clean the lino when you're done!" His muffled voice sounded from behind the closed door. "It's gonna stain!"

Ruby stood there for a long moment, the exhaustion of the whole affair settling deep. With a groan, she trudged past the dead body into the lounge and picked her phone up from the floor. She ignored the smear of blood she left on the screen as she unlocked it.

Then she slid down the wall back in the kitchen, to sit on the floor beside the man's head. His vacant eyes were still staring at the ceiling. She leaned her head against the wall, opened Instagram, and began to scroll with her right thumb. Tessa's face, grinning, a drink in each hand. *BEST. NIGHT. EVA!* Swipe. A boomerang of people drinking from goon bags. Swipe. A blurry group shot where everyone looked sweaty and happy. *Ugh.* Swipe.

With her left hand, she reached out and took hold of the man's outstretched arm. The skin was all clammy and gross now. She positioned his hand, limp and compliant, and brought it closer to her mouth. Her thumb flicked up on the phone's screen. An ad for university. She swore her internet searches were being watched. She should really study soon. God, she wasn't hungry at all. She was so tired. Then she opened her mouth and bit down on his index finger. There was a sharp, clean crack as her teeth met the bone. It was louder than the Skrillex song leaking from a video on her phone's feed. At least the music at the party sounded shit. She chewed with determination, the way one might chew past a tough piece of steak gristle, her eyes never leaving the bright glowing screen.

One scroll, one chew. Another photo of Tessa, this time with Bryce from the footy team, his arm draped possessively around her. Ruby swallowed. If she kissed Bryce, she was going to be so pissed. One finger down. She shifted her grip, moving to the next one. *BZZZZT.* A DM this time.

TESSA: U AWAKE BABE?? PARTY'S DEAD NOW, BUT MISSED U OMG!!! SEND ME A SELFIE SO I KNOW UR ALIVE LMFAO

Ruby glanced at herself in the black mirror of the oven door. Blood on her chin, a bit of something stuck in her teeth. She angled the phone, made sure only the top half of her face was in frame, and took the pic. Added a filter, the one that made everyone look soft and a little bit tanned.

QUIET NIGHT, she typed. TELL U ABOUT IT TMRW X

She put the phone down, shifted her grip on the dead man's wrist, and got back to work.

X

Ninna Nanna

The Eye Like a Strange Balloon Mounts Toward Infinity by Odilon Redon (1882)

I.
Melbourne rain, electric and blue.
Years since food was fresh,
Decades since the air was clean.
A century since anybody could discern
day,
for
night.
Gina sits in her seventy-first-floor apartment,
wearing the mesh suit,
one hundred nodes,
pressing against her skin
like her lovers who never existed.
At the bar (that isn't really a bar)
her colleagues laugh (they aren't really laughing)
and she drinks (the beer is real, at least)
warm in her actual hand,
while her digital hand holds nothing in THE VEIL).
Then after goodbyes,
Avatars fade,
logging off.
Try to sleep.
The next morning.
She maps places she will never go,
Places she has never been.
Today: southern Italy.
Render the stones.
Click, map, tap, tap.
Texture the light.
Click, turn, map, tap.
Feed the algorithm.
Let tourists walk through Mondragone,
from their living rooms in Singapore,

from their bedrooms in Sydney,
their meshes warming with faux Mediterranean sun.
But,
her screen glitches.
Strange.
Not right.
Superiors will be angry. Superiors will call.
Fix it. Now.
A pixel stutter in the cave systems northeast of town.
Coordinates that don't align.
Shadow where shadow shouldn't be.
That's an error.
She zooms in.
The data corrupts,
melts,
reforms.
Gina feels watched.
Not paranoia.
Watched.
Through the screen.
Through the numbers.
Something looking back,
through the coordinates:
Latitude,
longitude
depth,
like an address,
like a name,
like an invitation.

II.
She has family there.
Had family.
Great-grandmother's sister or cousin,
some thread of Italian blood she's never followed.
The feeling blooms:

I should go.
No.
I need to go.
The company approves the funding.
Ground-truthing. Quality assurance. The glitch needs
verification.
But that's not why.
Not really.
She books the flight.

III.
Italy is loud.
Italy is still very,
painfully,
loudly,
humidly,
human.
The taxi driver speaks and she can't understand,
her translator earpiece whines, fails,
gives her half-words,
fragments: *cave...old...don't...*
She smiles.
Nods.
Pays too much.
The air smells like rocks,
and exhaust,
and bread.
Real bread.
When did she last smell real bread?
The hotel is small.
The door requires a key.
An actual key. Metal. Strange.
She laughs alone in the room.
That night she tries The Veil,
the mesh suit connects,
but the lag is terrible,

her colleagues glitch and stutter,
their faces smear.
She takes it off.
Drinks the local beer (real)
from the minibar (real)
and sleeps (really sleeps)
for the first time in months.

IV.

Morning.
Market square.
A child, maybe six,
watches Gina fumble with paper money.
The child sings, soft:
OCCHIO CHE GUARDA, OCCHIO CHE VEDE
CONTA I BATTITI, UNO, DUE, TRE
Gina doesn't speak Italian well enough.
Her translator catches:
Eye...counting...sleep...
She smiles at the child.
The child doesn't smile back.
L'OCCHIO RIMANE SEMPRE APERTO.
The eye remains forever open.

V.

The cave is an hour's walk from town.
No signs.
No tourist infrastructure.
Just locals who know.
An old woman at the trailhead grabs Gina's wrist:
"Non andare. Non guardare."
Don't go. Don't look.
Gina pulls away gently.
Says: "I have to. For work."
The woman spits. Prays.

VI.

The cave mouth is ordinary.
Dark. Damp.
Cool air breathing out.
Her camera records.
Her scanner pings.
The data is wrong here too,
measurements that contradict themselves,
depth readings that claim the cave goes
down
twelve meters
and also infinite,
both true,
both real.
She enters.

VII.

At first it's easy.
Headlamp.
Steady ground.
She's mapping,
measuring,
trying to find where the glitch originates.
The passage narrows.
She
crouches.
The
ceiling
lowers.
She
crawls.
Her breathing echoes
 strange,
too many
echoes,
sound swallowed wrong.

VIII.

She tries to turn around.
Can't.
The space behind her has...
closed?
No.
Not closed.
Smaller.
The rock has moved
or she has moved
or space itself has folded.
Panic in her chest.
Forward.
Only forward.
The tunnel narrows.
She has to exhale to fit.
Shoulders scraping.
Her camera cracks against stone,
screen dark.
The walls are wet.
No.
Warm.
The stone is warm and wet and...

IX.

She sees it.
Ahead.
In the narrowest part,
where the passage should end,
where she'll be stuck,
where she'll die:
An eye.
Massive.
Bloodshot.
Wet.
Open.

Wider than her body.
Pupil black as space.
Veins threading like roots,
like rivers, like maps,
and the iris,
Looking at her,
looking into her,
looking through,
She blinks.

X.

The world shifts.
She's still in the cave.
Still pressed against wet stone.
Still staring at the eye.
But,
time has moved.
How long was her blink?
Half a second?
How long here?
She doesn't know.
Can't know.
Blinks again.
No, don't...
Too late.
The air is different.
Staler.
Her muscles ache.
Hours?
Days?
The eye doesn't blink.
Never blinks.
Counts hers.
Years.

XI.

OCCHIO CHE GUARDA
She tries not to blink.
CONTA I BATTITI
Eyes burning.
Drying.
UNO, DUE, TRE
Tears streaming.
She blinks.
Blinks.
Blinks.
The world outside is aging.
She knows it.
Can feel it in the air,
in the rot of her clothes,
in the way her hair has grown,
in the way her bones feel weak,
in the way her skin feels loose,
in the hunger that isn't hunger anymore,
just emptiness,
years of emptiness
compressed
into
the
space
between
her
eyelids
closing
and
opening
closing
and
opening.

XII.
She screams.
Claws at her face.

If she can't blink,
if there are no eyes to blink.
Her fingers find the sockets.
Digs.
The pain is hot
beautiful,
Real pain.
The first real feeling since the mesh suit,
since the glitched coordinates
that led her here,
that picked her,
that wanted her.
No.
Not wanted.
Just was.
She was.
She is.
There's nothing else to it.
Blood.
Still in the cave.
Still in front of the eye.
She is blind.

XIII.

Can't see,
but feels the eye watching.
the child singing
OCCHIO CHE GUARDA
Melbourne electric blue
but that was
years ago
decades
centuries?

                        she is still here still in the

narrowing
          still pressed against

Gina.
Not her voice.

XIV.

Gina died four thousand years ago.
Gina died when she blinked the seventh time.
Gina never existed.
You thought this was her story.

XV.

You.

yes, you,

reading this,

You thought you were safe.

You thought this was fiction.

Let me tell you about the cave.

Let me tell you about the narrowing.

Let me tell you about the girl who came

because the coordinates glitched

because I made them

glitch because I

AM

and she WAS

XVI.

I have been here since before Rome.

I will be here when the sun goes black.

I have counted the blinks.

Not hers.

Mine.

Yours.

XVII.

OCCHIO
    CHE   GUARDA
    CONTA I BATTITI

the mesh suit the glitch the cave the
blink no blink
the city is overgrown
The ash of people
Fluttering like a birds's wing
she wanted to map me to render me
to texture the light
but I am not data
I am not coordinates
I am the space between
closed and open

XVIII.

uno due tre
she dug her eyes out
thinking that would save her
    silly
precious   *little*   *girl*
I don't need her eyes
    I   have   mine
and mine are always
                always

                        Open

XIX.

The tiles press hard

Against her   back

Daniel stayed
on his knees

in the confessional and

let himself feel it.

Paige,

the receptionist,   was a twenty-something

The stick-together families are happier by far,

XX.
Do you feel it?
The narrowing?
Blink for me.
The page is a cave and you are crawling and behind you
the words have closed

    i've had trouble
      sleeping
lately
you cannot go back to page one
Blink.
Blink now.

you can only
read

         Forward

Do your eyes burn for me?

XXI.
OCCHIO CHE GUARDA, OCCHIO CHE VEDE

I see you.
CONTA I BATTITI, UNO, DUE, TRE
I'm counting.
QUANDO CHIUDI GLI OCCHI PER DORMIRE
When you close your eyes
L'OCCHIO RIMANE SEMPRE APERTO
I'll still be open.

XXII.

She is part of the cave now.

Part of the stone.

Her bones are sediment.
Her blood is inside

this page

Your eyes.
They Blink.
Her blood is the wet warmth you
feel
And you

you read this far

you thought you'd find an ending.

XXIII.

    I will wait, I have waited for longer than your

language exists

I watched the sun form

    watched the first cell split
watched the

species crawl from

water and I will watch you close this book and

OCCHIO CHE GUARDA OCCHIO CHE VEDE
CONTA I BATTITI UNO DUE TRE
L'OCCHIO RIMANE SEMPRE   APERTO

and   *blink*

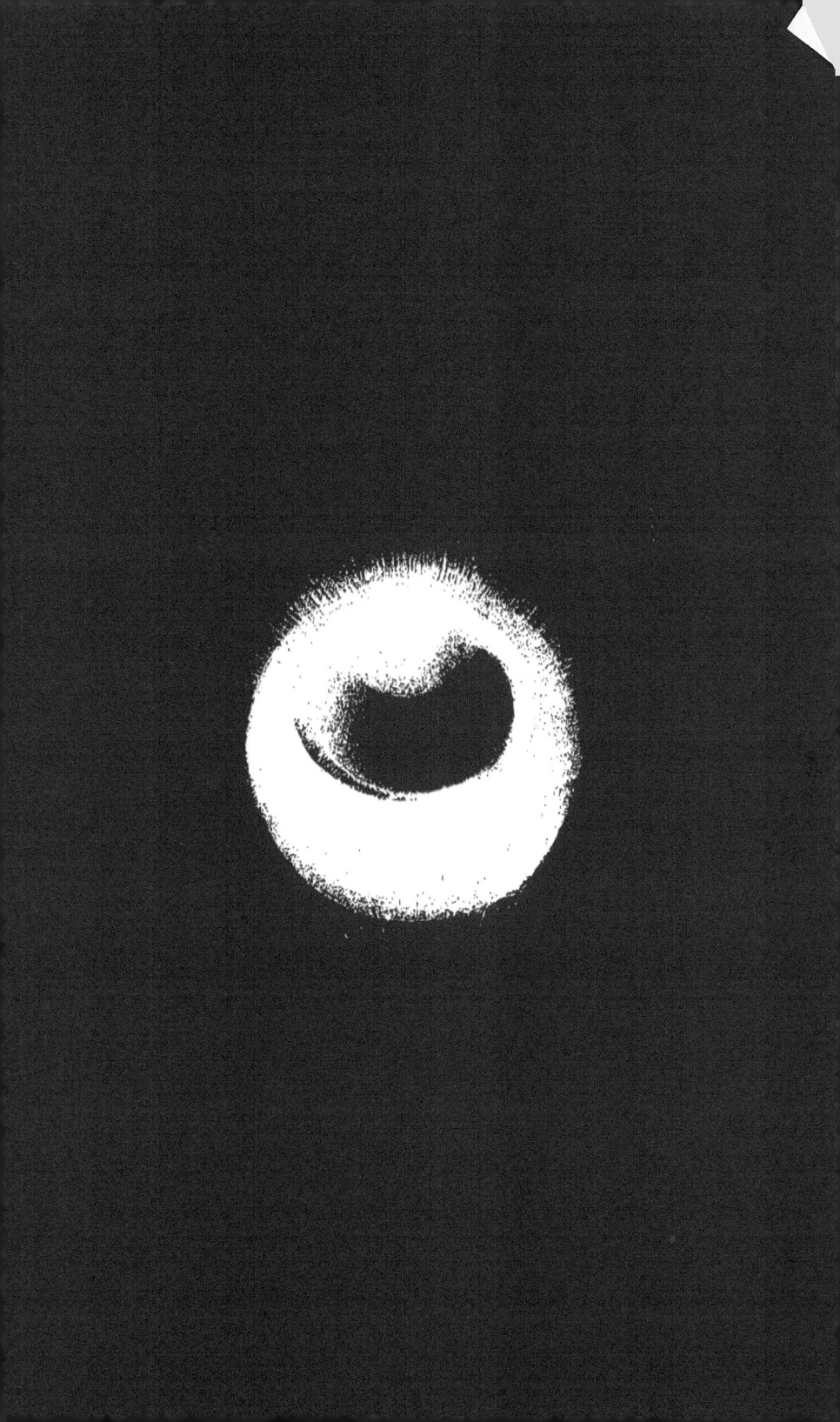